THE
SECRET
IN THE
STONES

YEARLING BOOKS are designed especially to entertain and enlighten young people. Patricia Reilly Giff, consultant to this series, received her bachelor's degree from Marymount College and a master's degree in history from St. John's University. She holds a Professional Diploma in Reading and a Doctorate of Humane Letters from Hofstra University. She was a teacher and reading consultant for many years, and is the author of numerous books for young readers.

THE
SECRET
IN THE
STONES

*TALES OF THE
NINE CHARMS*
Book 2

Erica Farber
and
J. R. Sansevere

A YEARLING BOOK

Published by
Dell Yearling
an imprint of
Random House Children's Books
a division of Random House, Inc.
1540 Broadway
New York, New York 10036

Visit us on the Web! www.randomhouse.com/kids

Educators and librarians, for a variety of teaching tools, visit us at
www.randomhouse.com/teachers

ISBN 0-440-41516-0

Printed in the United States of America

July 2001

10 9 8 7 6 5 4 3 2 1

OPM

For my father
—E.S.F.

Special thanks to L.
—E.S.F. AND J.R.S.

Nine were the charms,
golden-silver, made of light,
forged by the Lords of Time
to help take back the night.
Each of these nine lords
one color charm did hold,
to fight the darkness rising,
or so the story's told.

But long ago the nine were lost,
the Lords of Time all passed.
Dark and light made an uneasy truce,
but never would that last.
One must find the nine,
one must have the power,
and one will come from somewhere else
to fight the Dark Lord's hour.

Silver will be his sword,
silver like his eyes.
The choosing of the charms
is where his skill lies.

Sign of the Dragon's Eye,
great will be her sight.
She is the Protector,
the guardian of the light.
From another world
where magic is no more,
his task shall be to fight
for the light in the coming war.
Called by all the Bearer,
the white dragon holds the key
to find the Chooser and Protector
and form the Circle of Three.

But if a second Bearer
by the dark is then called forth,
the black dragon shall be freed
from its prison in the North.
And the Bearer of the Dark
shall face the Bearer of the Light.
The white dragon must be risen
or all shall be endless night.

—The Lost Books of the Dragon Kings
a Fragment of the Prophecy

 # PROLOGUE

Zoe Ryder hurried along the hallway, her pale blue eyes fastened on a bulging red knapsack that was fast disappearing around the corner ahead of her.

"Wait up!" she called, her chunky-heeled black sandals clacking on the shiny linoleum as she struggled to push her way, without slipping, through the Friday afternoon crowd of seventh- and eighth-graders all rushing to leave school. Her stepmother was right about these shoes. They weren't practical, but they looked great, especially with her new long black dress. And that was definitely worth it, as far as Zoe was concerned.

"See you tonight, Zoe!" called some seventh-grade girls, gathered in a group around one locker.

Zoe waved absently and hurried around the corner,

flipping her dark bangs out of her eyes. She didn't stop. She couldn't lose that knapsack. Zoe Ryder was nothing if not determined, especially when it came to getting her own way.

"Wait for me!" she called again as the knapsack surged into view just a few yards away.

"I've been waiting all year," Todd Randall said with a laugh.

"In your dreams," she called over her shoulder as she careened along the hall. As if she would ever go out with a boy her own age, even Todd, who all the girls in her class agreed was the best-looking guy in the entire junior high.

"Wait!" she tried again, running out into the June sunshine, squinting down at the skinny, stoop-shouldered girl who was halfway down the school's front steps. "Megan! Wait!"

The girl turned, pushing her thick, dark-rimmed glasses up further on her freckled nose as she stared at Zoe in total shock.

"Hey, Megan," Zoe said with a big smile. "I've been trying to catch up with you ever since the bell rang."

"Hi," murmured the shy girl, a dark red blush crawling from her neck to her face.

"So, what's up?" Zoe asked, moving down next to her as throngs of middle schoolers poured out of the building.

Megan Landers bit her lip and shook her head, scuffing one muddy brown loafer into the cement. Loafers, Zoe thought. What mom shoes. Megan sure was a nerd, especially with those silly horse buttons she had plastered all over her knapsack. Horseback riding was so elementary school.

"I was wondering," Zoe went on in the sweet voice she used on her mother when she wanted to borrow her credit card, "if you wanted to go to the movies tonight."

"I—I don't . . . know," Megan answered, chewing on the end of a red braid—just like a little kid, Zoe thought. How disgusting.

"Come on," she continued brightly. "It'll be fun."

"I don't know. I have a lot of homework."

"So what? It's Friday night. You have all weekend to do your homework."

Megan nodded but didn't say anything as the girls continued down the steps.

"Thing is, we'll need a ride. I'm spending the weekend at my dad's, just down the road from you. But he's busy. Do you think maybe someone in your family could take us?" Zoe paused for a minute, as if considering something. "Hey, what about your brother? It's so much more fun if you don't have to involve parents."

"Shane?"

Zoe nodded, thinking, Duh, who else? And at that

moment, just as she had calculated, a black BMW came into view. "Ask him," Zoe urged. "Come on. That's him right now, isn't it?"

Megan stood for a moment, sucking on her hair again.

"Come on, Megan. It'll be fun. You can hang with me and my friends. You'll have a great time. I promise." What was a little lie? Zoe thought. It didn't matter, just like that Italian dude they'd studied in history had written. Machia*something*. The end justifies the means. And getting a chance to talk to Shane Landers was definitely an end that justified doing most anything.

At six that night Zoe and Megan stood on the three-sided wraparound porch of the Landers's colonial home, listening to the hum of an engine and the crunch of gravel. Seconds later, the BMW came to a stop. Even though Zoe was trying hard to seem older than her thirteen years, she couldn't stop staring at Shane. He was gorgeous with a capital *G*, with blond hair all wet and curly from soccer practice and his green eyes crinkling at the corners. Jen and Ashley would die when they saw her. Just totally die. It had been worth the whole afternoon of hanging out with nerdy, annoying Megan and her boring collection of horse figurines.

Megan moved toward the passenger door, which brought Zoe to her senses. No way was she going to lose this golden opportunity to nerd girl. Gently she nudged Megan out of the way.

"Sorry, Meg," she gushed in a voice so sweet you could practically hear the sugar dripping. "But I get carsick if I sit in the back."

"Hey, Squirt," Shane said, smiling at his sister. "Who's your friend?"

Zoe's stomach flip-flopped. "I'm Zoe," she cut in, opening the car door. "Zoe Ryder. My dad lives down the road."

"Royal Ryder's your dad?"

"Uh-huh," Zoe answered, settling herself into the smooth leather upholstery and buckling the seat belt.

"Cool. My parents said his latest show was great."

Zoe nodded as Shane guided the car down the curving driveway and onto the bumpy country road. A flash of heat lightning lit up the sky, turning the hot June night an electric purple.

"Ooh," Zoe murmured, looking sideways at Shane, who was lounging back against the seat with one hand on the wheel. "A storm."

"Yeah, but it's not supposed to break until later."

"So, how's soccer going?" She knew that boys loved to talk about sports and figured it was a sure way to keep him interested.

"Excellent," Shane said, going on to tell her all about

the high school team and the games they'd won and the big tournament coming up that summer in Colorado. Zoe oohed and aahed and flipped her hair, her heart soaring. Shane Landers was actually talking to her. It wasn't until Megan pointed out that the movie theater was just around the corner that Zoe remembered Shane's sister was even in the car.

"Thanks so much for the ride, Shane," Zoe said, simpering at him, her blue eyes sparkling. She glanced out the car window at the sidewalk thronged with kids, looking for a sign of Ashley or Jen.

"No problem," Shane said.

Megan clambered out of the backseat just as Zoe spotted her friends. She jiggled the door handle a few times, but the door wouldn't open.

"Gee, Shane, I don't know what—"

"I'll get it," he said. "I don't know why it's sticking."

I do, Zoe thought as Shane made his way over to her side of the car. She pulled out the wad of gum she'd stuck in the door handle just moments earlier.

"Thanks, Shaaaane," she crowed as he opened her door with a flourish.

She watched with pleasure as heads turned. She actually saw Ashley's and Jen's mouths drop open. "See you."

"Peace," Shane said, climbing back into the car. "Have fun, Squirt."

Megan and Zoe waved as the BMW disappeared down the street.

"I can't believe—," Jen began.

"Shane Landers!" Ashley exclaimed. "*The* Shane Landers. Incredible."

"I know," Zoe said, grinning triumphantly.

"We better get going," Jen said, waving three tickets. "The movie's about to start."

"Um . . . ," Megan began, scuffing one loafer along the sidewalk.

"Let's go," Zoe mouthed to Ashley and Jen. Then she turned to Megan. "Sorry. But they only got a ticket for me. They didn't know you were coming. I guess you'll have to wait in line for yours. You don't mind, right?"

Zoe watched as Megan trained her thick glasses on the line that snaked halfway down the block.

"Sorry," Zoe said again as her two friends rolled their eyes. "We'll wait for you inside."

"As if," Ashley murmured.

"We'll save a seat," Zoe called over her shoulder.

And she turned away and headed after her friends, but not before she'd seen the telltale glistening in Megan's eyes and the quivering lower lip. What a crybaby, Zoe thought. It wasn't her fault her friends hadn't bought enough tickets.

After the movie Jen's mother drove Zoe to her dad's house. She pushed open the antique front door and crossed the spacious foyer, stepping over the Oriental rug, trying not to think about how it had once graced the floor of the dining room of the house where she now lived alone with her mother. She kicked a toy out of her way, a plastic robot thing that hit the stone fireplace with a bang. She hoped it had broken. Serve the brats right for leaving it out.

"Hello!" she called.

There was no answer. Just the drone of the television set from the playroom.

"Hello!" she called again, stomping through the kitchen. A half-eaten pizza was on the table. Her stepmother was no kind of housekeeper. At least Zoe's mother had the sense to have a maid. Not Lisa. She claimed she liked to cook and even to clean. Zoe didn't believe that for one minute. Secretly she thought Lisa was just afraid of having a maid because she didn't come from money and had no clue how to manage one.

Just another reason Zoe was sure her father's second marriage would never last.

Through the French doors she saw her father sitting on the steps of the pool. Trevor was in the water on one side of him and Devon on the other. Lisa sat opposite, wearing her ugly green-and-gold one-piece suit with the little skirt. She had the worst taste in clothes.

"Hi, Dad," she said, pretending not to see the others.

But Trevor had chosen just that moment to choke on a mouthful of water. Four-year-olds were such pains, Zoe thought.

"Hi, Zoe," Lisa answered instead, as Zoe's dad patted Trevor on the back. "How was the movie?"

She sure is good, Zoe thought. Her smile seemed so genuine, but Zoe knew the truth. Lisa couldn't stand having her around. It was the Cinderella principle, wasn't it?

"Good," Zoe answered curtly, turning her back.

"Well, your brothers really missed you."

Zoe rolled her eyes. "They're not my brothers," she muttered under her breath, just loud enough for Lisa to hear.

"The movie was about a mummy, wasn't it?" Lisa continued, still smiling as if Zoe hadn't said anything rude or obnoxious.

Even though it was, Zoe wasn't about to talk to Lisa about it. "Dad," she began again, "I saw this—"

"Alley-alley-oop!" her father boomed, tossing Devon up in the air, then catching him just as he hit the water.

Devon squealed in delight. Zoe frowned and turned away, clomping up the deck steps away from the pool.

"Zoe! Where are you going?" It was Lisa's voice, sounding warm and concerned, like the big bad wolf when he tricked Red Riding Hood. It was phony. Totally phony, and Zoe wasn't buying.

Zoe didn't even turn around.

"Zoe! It's about to storm. I don't think you should be going anywhere."

"I don't have to listen to you," Zoe called over her shoulder, her smile as big and fake as Lisa's. "You're not my mother, you know."

With that, she turned the corner and scrambled over the old stone wall that ran the perimeter of the property. She crossed the road, deserted at this time of night, and headed for the empty house opposite. It was dark, but Zoe could see well enough in the moonlight. Anyhow, she knew the way. As she walked through the overgrown grass past the gnarled old apple trees, she thought about Lisa and the twins and how much she wished they would just disappear. Then her life could return to the way it used to be.

She pursed her lips in determination as she wriggled between two overgrown trees into the clearing behind the house. When she came to the spring-fed pond, she stepped carefully along the mossy stones. The pond was a dark murky green and filled with lily pads. Bullfrogs croaked, and she could hear the gurgling of the stream and, listening closely, the echo of ghostly laughter from her father's house across the street.

She wasn't sure why she'd come here. The place was kind of creepy, especially the stone one-winged angel that sat at the edge of the pool. Why would someone keep something that was broken, anyway?

In the distance thunder rumbled. Lightning streaked the sky. Zoe shivered. The storm was getting closer. She should go home if she didn't want to get wet, but she didn't feel like going back yet. A sudden splash to her right made her jump. It was just a frog, but as she stared, something glinting on the mossy stones caught her eye.

Curious, Zoe got to her feet. She knew the house had once belonged to some wealthy New Yorkers back in the Roaring Twenties—flappers who threw wild parties, drank tons of champagne, and danced until dawn in their sheer sequined dresses. Zoe would have liked to have been a beautiful flapper living in luxury. Maybe the shining thing was a piece of jewelry left behind by a flapper after a romantic tryst.

Her imagination running wild, Zoe bent to pick up the shiny trinket. It felt light in her hand, made of some metal that was not quite silver and not quite gold. It had strange designs carved all over it, but the most amazing thing was the stone in the center. It was a very pale blue that glittered like an icicle in winter sun, casting a bright bluish light. Zoe had never seen anything like it. It was old, she was sure of it. Not just decades old, but centuries old.

A crack of thunder made her jump. It felt as if it had struck right over her head. Suddenly she became very aware of how small and alone she was out in the dark. The air hung thick and steamy around her. It was going to rain any second. She scrambled to her feet as a jagged fork of purple white lightning lit up the sky.

Everything after that happened very quickly, like a movie on fast-forward. She had only taken a few steps when she heard an earsplitting crack and smelled something burning. She looked up in horror as a huge branch came hurtling toward the pond. As she jumped backward, her sandals slipped on the mossy stones and she fell into the water.

A scream froze in her throat as she scrabbled wildly, trying to pull herself out of the murky water. But her hands grasped nothing but the slimy stones, and then she began to sink into darkness. The water closed over her head. Wildly she wondered how she could be sinking. There was no current in the pond, and she knew how to swim.

Futilely she struggled to pull herself out of the water. It was as if invisible hands were dragging her down, pulling her farther and farther from the stormy night.

She kept falling and falling until she realized with a start that she wasn't even in water anymore. Air rushed past her ears, making a whining, whistling sound.

After a time Zoe gave up struggling and allowed her body to simply fall, faster and faster, deeper and deeper into the inky black darkness. . . .

CHAPTER I

Aurora opened her eyes, blinking in the sunlight. She was lying on a cold stone floor. The room was dark but for one shaft of light slanting across her face. She sat up slowly, wondering where she was. Wooden shelves filled with books lined the walls. In the center of the room was a table carved of smooth white wood, cut in an ancient style with thick tree-trunk legs and curved feet. She'd never seen anything like it, but white wood like that came only from the North. The North. She couldn't be in the North, though. It was too warm. Standing, she made her way over to the table, trying to get her bearings. Her head hurt and her mouth was dry and gritty, as if it were filled with sand.

Sand. The desert. She remembered being in the desert, riding on horseback across endless desert sands.

Riding through the day and the night until she lost track of time. But why? Where had she been going in such a hurry?

She saw the food on the table at the same time that her stomach rumbled, the sound loud in the silence of the dusty, book-filled room. She was so hungry, she couldn't remember when she'd eaten last. She broke off a piece of stale bread and stuffed it in her mouth, along with a hunk of cheese. There was a glass decanter filled with something clear that looked like water. She picked it up and was about to drink when she stopped, her gaze riveted on a black engraving in the center of the table. It was a dragon. A black dragon with red eyes and a long, scaly tail, its mouth belching a stream of fire.

Memories came flooding back. Jah capturing her at the Palace of Sand and Stone, seizing the pouch with the nine charms of the Lords of Time and bringing her here to the House of the Black Rock, the Dragons' secret training camp in the desert. Aurora bit her lip, studying the engraving, unable to take her eyes away from its lashing tail and fierce, jutting fangs. She shivered despite the warmth of the room. If only she hadn't lost Niko. None of this might have happened and the charms might still be safe. And Niko, too. What kind of protector was she? She had to find the charms.

She studied the room, trying to figure out her best possible escape route. It was five sided, with doors in three of the walls, and one tiny window. She tried the handles of all three doors, but they were locked. Sighing in frustration, she approached the bookshelves and ran a finger over the smooth leather spines, squinting to read some of the titles: *Geographie of the Fixed Stars, The Lost Books of the Dragon Kings, Magick of the Skyggni.*

Just then she heard footsteps. She threw herself under the table, crouching in the shadows as the door on the left swung open.

"Are you sure this is a good idea, Marcus?" a high, thin voice asked, and Aurora saw three pairs of legs—dressed identically in white pants topped with tunics—enter the room. "Not that I'm scared or nothin', but if General Da Gama catches us, we're fish bait."

"What are you talking about?" a gruff voice shot back. "You backing out, Bram?"

"No, Marcus." It was the high, thin voice. "Uh . . . I just thought we should be careful, that's all. I mean, we're in enough trouble as it is."

Aurora tensed as one of the boys slammed into the table.

"You thought? Who cares what you thought. After all the trouble it took to steal the key, you wanna back out now?"

"No, Marcus, I'm with you."

"You sure?" cut in the third boy, speaking for the first time. Then he apparently delivered a massive punch to Bram's stomach. Aurora tensed again as Bram coughed and his legs doubled up. "You listen to Marcus," the boy said. "He's the one that does the talkin'. Got it, punk?"

Bram staggered away from the table.

"The way I see it, we gotta find a map of the desert." Marcus's voice was harsh and insistent, the tone of a bully used to getting his way. "There's gotta be maps in here. It *is* a library. Then we gotta figure out where those two went."

"Hey look, food," said the third boy.

The boys crowded around the table and shoved themselves onto the benches. Aurora made herself as small as possible as legs dangled down on her left and her right.

"The way I see it," Marcus mumbled through a mouthful of cheese and bread, "is that those two rode out of here on that wild horse right into the desert."

"Right," murmured the other two.

"I bet they died," Bram ventured.

"No they didn't, stupid," Marcus shot back. "No, that strange kid—what's his name?"

"You mean that new recruit?" the third boy said. "Name's Niko, I think."

Aurora's heart began to beat fast in her chest. Niko?

"No, not him. The other one who said that red charm I found was his."

Aurora was so shocked she felt as if all the air had been sucked out of her. These boys knew about the red charm, the one that Niko had chosen, the one she had sent out to call forth the Bearer.

"Yeah, he's the one who took a swing at you. Remember, Marcus?" Bram babbled.

"What are you talking about?" Marcus countered contemptuously. "I beat that kid up real good."

"Yeah, you did," agreed the third boy. "His name was Walker, I remember now."

"Walker, that's it. See, what I think happened is, that kid, Walker, rode that wild black horse, and then saved the other kid, Niko. And the reason I know them two didn't die is cuz I heard Jah talking to General Da Gama. Actually, Da Gama was doin' most of the talkin', since Jah don't never say much."

"Nope."

"He's so weird," Bram added. "They say he smiled when he walked over the flaming fires during his ceremony to become a Dragon. Smiled, can you believe it? So what'd Da Gama say, Marcus?"

"He said Niko and that kid Walker went through some door that opened right up in the middle of the desert."

"A door in the desert? Where? In the air?"

"You hard of hearin', or something? That's what Da Gama said."

"So what's the plan?" asked the third boy.

"If we could get that charm," Marcus said, "I bet Lord Draco would make us Dragons cuz he wants that thing so bad. All's we gotta do is find that door, go through it and get Niko and Walker."

"Bet it's not that easy," Bram said softly.

Marcus jumped up. He must have grabbed Bram's collar and twisted it because Aurora could hear Bram choking. "You don't, do you? Well, I wasn't askin' you, was I?"

"Marcus is right," the third boy said. "If those two could do it, so can we."

There was silence around the table. Marcus threw himself back onto the bench, his foot jabbing Aurora hard in the ribs. Before she could stop herself, she let out a small yelp.

"What was that?"

"One of you fraidycats meowing?"

"Wasn't me."

Seconds passed. None of the boys moved. Aurora was just beginning to feel safe when rough hands pulled her from beneath the table, yanking her dress so hard she was afraid it would rip. Marcus yanked her upright and she found herself staring up into dark, menacing eyes. He was younger than she had thought. No more than fourteen or so, but big for his age.

"It's a girl," Bram exclaimed incredulously.

"No way," added the other boy. "There's no girls at Black Rock."

"Well, there are now," Aurora said, trying to stand her ground and sound tough.

"What are you doin' eavesdroppin' on our private conversation?" Marcus said. He tightened his hold, making her gasp for air.

"Let me go," Aurora said. "Anyway, I'm not the one who snuck in here, am I?"

Marcus scowled at her, his dark eyes smoldering.

"If you don't let me go, I'll tell Lord Draco that you stole the key."

"You would not!"

"I would unless you do something for me."

"What?" Bram asked.

"Shut up, stupid," Marcus yelled. "We don't have to bargain with her. She's in our power, not the other way around."

"Tell me the way out of here and I'll keep my mouth shut. Otherwise I might just have to start screaming. And then who knows who might come running?"

Marcus laughed scornfully. "Quit threatenin' me, you stupid girl. You're the one's locked up in here, not us. The thing I wanna know is why. I got this feelin' that it's got somethin' to do with those two that got away."

Aurora tried hard not to betray her surprise at Marcus's insight. He wasn't as stupid as he looked. "Let me go and maybe I'll tell you."

Marcus released his hold on her collar so fast she went sprawling into the two other boys. "Get off me!" she said through her teeth, pushing them away.

"She's like a wildcat," Bram said.

"Yeah, one that's been out in the garbage dump, cuz she smells pretty bad," put in the third boy. All three of them laughed.

Aurora positioned herself in front of Marcus and stared into his eyes. She made herself breathe slowly in and out and willed her beating heart to still so that she could concentrate.

"What are you doin'?"

"I'm going to show you something," Aurora said slowly, making her voice sound as provocative as possible.

"What?"

"You'll see. Just be very quiet." Her breathing quickened, her eyes never leaving Marcus's face. It had to work. It was the only way. Air in one nostril and out the other, blanking out her thoughts like a white sheet draped across her mind's eye. Slowly she began to feel the telltale tingling in her forehead and the sweat trickling down her neck. She reached out with her mind and entered Marcus's thoughts. She saw his secret worries about being caught, his distrust of his friends, an image of a woman with dark eyes like Marcus's, holding a baby and cowering as a big man stumbled toward her, and—

Suddenly something hard and black slammed down in front of her eyes. Aurora gasped and reeled backward, clutching her head as though she'd been hit.

"The untrained mind cannot possibly do battle against the trained, Gypsy girl." The voice was deep and resonant, reverberating in the small room.

A man dressed in a long red robe had entered the chamber. His face was half in shadow, half in light, accentuating the sharpness of his chin and cheekbones. Behind him the boys stood frozen, their expressions tense and scared. Even Marcus.

"Sorry, Lord Draco, sir," they intoned, bowing.

But Lord Draco didn't even acknowledge them. His black eyes burned into Aurora's. "How did these three novices get in here?" he asked.

Aurora bit her lip and shook her head, refusing to answer. Lord Draco's mind probed hers like a knife slicing through a wedge of cheese, and she was powerless to keep him out of her thoughts.

Lord Draco turned and smiled at the three boys.

"The punishment for stealing a key is severe. Now be gone, all of you. General Da Gama awaits you beyond the door."

Marcus shot Aurora a look that made it clear he thought their getting caught was all her fault. She watched as the boys shuffled silently out of the room, leaving her alone with Lord Draco.

"Step closer and raise your right hand."

Trembling, Aurora took a few tentative steps. Lord Draco's expression was so forbidding it didn't even cross her mind not to obey. Slowly she raised her right hand. The strange, dark triangular shape stood out against the paleness of her skin.

"The Dragon's Eye, the sign of the Protector," he said.

Aurora tried to hang on to her thoughts, but it was as if her head were filled with soup, not brains.

"It is destiny, is it not? What else could have caused the nine charms of the Lords of Time to wind up in my possession? Or should I say eight, since you and the Chooser already sent out the red charm. And now here you are, the Protector of the charms. Though the Chooser and the Bearer have escaped, they, too, will end up where they belong. The charm of fire and blood will find its way back to the others. That, too, is destiny."

Lord Draco paused, his eyes glittering like black mirrors as they gazed into hers. "Where is the map of the Doors of the Hunab Ku, Protector?"

Aurora shook her head. "I don't know what you're talking about."

"Castor Le Croix, the foolish ambassador from Kasmania, let you get away with it. But you don't have it now. So where is it?"

Aurora said nothing.

"You leave me no choice, I'm afraid," Lord Draco said.

Before Aurora knew what was happening, she could feel his mind inside hers, probing, searching, sorting through the jumble of thoughts and memories. She tried to put up a wall, to think of something else, of her grandmother, Titi, and the Gypsy camp; of songs around the campfire; of her best friend, Romany; of her mother, who was long dead. But it was no use. Like a practiced pearl diver on the muddy ocean floor, Lord Draco prized the information out of her mind.

"A boy named Serge," Lord Draco murmured, his eyes never leaving her face. "A river rat. I see. So you dropped the map of the Doors of the Hunab Ku, back in the City of Sand and Stone. How very irresponsible of you, Protector, especially since the Empress herself had entrusted it to you."

Aurora, her mind reeling, just stood there, staring

dumbly at Lord Draco. Please, she thought, don't bring Serge any harm. He was just a boy she'd met by accident. He didn't know anything about who she really was and what was at stake.

"Now that I am regent of the young Emperor of Sunnebēam, you realize that I control the entire kingdom, especially with the Empress out of the way. . . ." Lord Draco let his words trail off meaningfully. "So don't expect anyone to come running to your rescue."

Aurora took a deep breath, trying to gather her scattered thoughts. If only she could think more clearly. She'd gone to the palace to help the Empress, that's why she'd been in the City of Sand and Stone, but she'd gotten there too late and had been captured. "What did you do to her?" Aurora finally asked.

"That is not your concern, nor mine any longer. Now that you are here, I feel the stirrings of the black dragon. Soon, soon he will rise as the prophecy foretold so long ago."

"That has nothing to do with me." Aurora choked out the words, trying not to look into Lord Draco's glittering eyes.

"Ah, but it does. In fact, none of this could happen without you." Lord Draco's voice was icy, menacing, sending a chill into Aurora's heart.

"What do you mean?" she whispered.

"All in time. You will be leaving tomorrow on a long

journey to a place more sacred to the nine charms and the Lords of Time than any other. A place on the far reaches of the Cold Edge. There you will fulfill a destiny older and greater than either of us, and the dark will finally gain what it once lost."

"I won't!" Aurora gasped. "I won't do anything for the dark."

"Come, Aurora, stop being so childish. Without the dark, there would be no light, and without the light, no shadows would fall and there would be no darkness. You are both light and dark yourself. Why do you think the old ones, those Gypsies with their old-fashioned and ineffectual magic tricks, distrusted you so? Because they could see in their limited fashion the darkness in your soul."

Aurora opened her mouth, but no words came out. She watched in silence as Lord Draco locked two of the doors and then disappeared through the third. Then she heard the telltale click as he locked the final door.

CHAPTER 2

"Would you please stop talking about how hungry you are," Niko snapped, his own stomach choosing just that moment to rumble. "Food is the least of our problems."

"Right," Walker said, rolling his eyes and letting out his breath in a long, exasperated sigh. "If we don't eat, we die. Remember? It's a fact of life and don't start telling me some long weird saga about superhero guys from your world. We need food. Plain and simple. End of story. Otherwise . . ."

Niko didn't say anything. There was nothing to say. Walker was right—they did need food. They hadn't eaten anything except a few berries since they'd gone through that glittering circle of lights into this world.

And that was at least two or three days ago. Not that Niko remembered anything very clearly from that night except for the fact that Walker had saved his life. If Walker hadn't dragged him into this world, he would have been buried alive by the furiously blowing sand. Or captured again by the Dragons.

"Listen, the way I've got it figured, it's pretty simple," Walker continued, scuffing his dirty high-tops into the dust of the mountain road. The two boys were winding their way down toward a town, which sat on the seashore. "Getting someone to give us food for no reason, except out of the goodness of their hearts, seems highly unlikely to me. I mean, look at us. We're a mess. And I'm pretty sure we stink."

Niko wrinkled his nose, blowing his long dark bangs out of his eyes. Walker was right about that too. His own tunic was in tatters and his bare feet crusted with dirt. Walker's white tunic had turned a dingy gray, one sleeve was torn clean off at the shoulder, and his face was covered with a thin brown film of dust.

"So that's out," Walker went on. "Which leaves us with two options. Either we figure out a way to steal some food, or we find a job and make some money so we can buy food."

"But food is not what's going to get us back to my

world," Niko burst out. "And getting back there is what matters most."

"Not if we're dead," Walker stated matter-of-factly, stepping around a huge black boulder that had appeared in the turning of the road. It was the size of a small house and pitted all over with shiny silver holes. It must have fallen recently because it wasn't covered in dust, like everything else in the mountains.

Niko stopped walking and reached out to touch the boulder. The bumpy surface felt warm. "A thunderstone," he murmured in wonder. "The master and I studied them. Some people believe that the falling of a thunderstone from the heavens means the end of the world. They also believe the stone itself has magic properties."

"What!" Walker sputtered, staring at Niko as if he'd sprouted two heads. "This is a meteorite. I saw one once on a class field trip to the science museum. It's the debris from a comet, just a bunch of space matter that condenses into this solid form when it falls into the coolness of the atmosphere. It has nothing to do with the world ending or magic or anything, believe me, or my world would have ended ages ago."

"Hmm," Niko said. "The master didn't believe the end-of-the-world theory either. He said it had something to do with dark matter, the particles swirling through space that we can't see but that keep the worlds in balance."

"That's funny," Walker said. "We call it dark matter, too."

The boys continued walking in silence. Although it was still early morning, the sun was hot and Niko could feel the sweat dripping down his back. He couldn't help thinking about his master, Lord Amber, and how much he would have enjoyed seeing this thunderstone with his very own eyes. The sadness gripped his heart once more, squeezing it till he felt as if he couldn't breathe.

"We've looked everywhere, but that door's gone." Walker's voice brought Niko back to the moment. "You know it is. And there's no way that door is ever going to appear again. Or maybe not no way, but the odds are so slim they're like nothing. We'll just have to figure out something else."

The door. That strange ring of lights that had appeared suddenly in the stormy desert night. Somehow, the opening had disappeared without a trace, leaving the two of them trapped in another world.

"I keep thinking about the charm," Walker said. "As far as I can see, it's our only hope. The thing is how to get it to work? There must be some trick to activate it, you know, some code or key or something."

Niko nodded wearily as they continued their descent. They'd gone over all this before—the charm with the fiery red center that he and Aurora had sent out. But that seemed so long ago. Aurora was gone now somewhere back in his world, with the eight other charms. She didn't even know that the ninth charm had worked and brought forth a Bearer. She would be surprised if she ever met Walker. He was like nothing she could ever have imagined, with the funny rubber-soled shoes he called high-tops and his strange way of speaking.

"Did you even hear what I said? Are you even listening?" Walker demanded.

Niko nodded, stepping carefully. The way was steeper here, rockier, but also greener, with trees and grass growing wildly. Below he could now make out the dark silhouettes of boats bobbing in the water and the pastel colors of the houses of the town.

"Well?" Walker asked.

"What?"

"What do you think?"

"About what?"

Walker shook his head. "You are so weird sometimes."

"Why? Because I don't talk if I have nothing to say?" Niko snapped.

Walker's blue eyes flashed as he rubbed some dirt out of his short blond hair in a gesture of frustration.

"I—I'm sorry," Niko stammered. "I didn't mean

anything. I'm just hungry, I guess, and it's made me irritable."

"You can say that again." Walker said with a grin, his teeth gleaming brightly in his dirty face. "See, I was right from the beginning. Food is our biggest problem. Admit it. I'm right."

He poked Niko in the arm.

"You're right," Niko agreed, smiling despite himself. That was one thing about Walker. No matter how terrible things were, he wouldn't stop arguing, and when he won an argument, it made him as happy as if he'd won a tournament or something.

Finally, the boys reached the town. It was quiet so early in the morning. Except for a few squalling seagulls hunting for food and some fishing boats being readied in the harbor, the area seemed deserted. The two boys headed toward the wide commercial boulevard that ran along the water, but there was no one about.

"Let's try over there," Walker said, pointing at a warren of twisting streets leading away from the harbor.

"I don't know," Niko said. "I think we should—"

"Look!" Walker interrupted. "A cart just disappeared around that corner. And I'm pretty sure there was food on it. Come on, let's go."

Walker sprinted away and Niko had no choice but to follow. When he caught up with his friend, they found themselves on a narrow, cobbled lane lined with tightly shuttered, thatch-roofed cottages built against one another. The rank odor of sewage permeated the air. As the boys rounded a corner into another mean, twisting street, the cottages gave way to ruins overgrown with weeds and completely deserted.

"You must have imagined the cart," Niko said, trying to catch his breath.

Walker shook his head. "There was fruit on it. I swear. Oranges and apples and—"

"Sounds to me like a hallucination created by the overwhelming hunger in your belly and your brain's—"

Niko never finished his sentence because at that moment they came upon a cart just like the one Walker had described. It was propped in front of a wooden door that, unlike others they had passed, actually hung securely on its hinges. It looked remarkably solid and well maintained, as did the two-story timbered cottage it fronted. Flowers grew all around, filling the air with a sweet, spicy scent. Walker had eyes only for the cart, or rather for its contents—fruits and vegetables. Before Niko could do anything, his friend picked up an apple and began to eat it.

"Stop!" Niko shouted. "You can't just take that apple without permission or payment. It's wrong."

Walker nodded, apple juice dribbling down his chin. "This is the best apple I ever had," he said, as if Niko hadn't spoken. "And I don't even like apples."

Niko shook his head. "You are impossible."

"Take one," Walker said. "You'll see what I mean. Stop being so uptight."

Niko let out his breath in an exasperated sigh and approached the door. "I will not take anything without asking first. It's barbaric and uncivilized. We call it stealing in my world."

"I don't think it's stealing when you're starving. I mean, how are we supposed to survive if we don't eat? And we have to survive because as you keep telling me I'm the Bearer and you're the Chooser and we have this huge destiny to fulfill or the dark will obliterate the light and then everything good in all the worlds will be destroyed. Right?"

Niko was barely listening, for as he stood in front of the door, he saw something that made him wonder if *he* were the one hallucinating. Carved beneath the iron door-knocker was a triangular symbol he knew only too well—although what it might be doing here he couldn't begin to imagine.

"What's with you, Mr. Morality?" Walker prodded.

"Cat got your tongue? Was my argument so convincing it took your breath away?"

"Hardly," Niko said, turning. "Come here and look at this."

Walker went over to where Niko stood and looked at the symbol. "So?"

"So? That is the sign of the Dragon's Eye. It's a sign of protection in my world."

"Your world?" a rasping voice said as the door swung open, revealing an old man with piercing blue eyes and long silver hair.

Both boys jumped back in surprise.

"Which world are you from?" the man prodded, peering at them with those intense eyes.

"Well, it's not exactly . . . ," Niko began as Walker said, "It's hard to say. . . ."

The old man laughed. "You think you are the first to come here from another world?" He looked at them with a mixture of disbelief and something kinder that might have been sympathy, then said to Niko, "Not so many years ago, I met someone else also familiar with the sign on my door. He, too, was a warrior like you, although he had a sword to prove it, a gleaming silver sword."

Niko frowned. "I don't know what you mean."

"I can see that," the old man said.

"We only wanted some fruit because we're starving and my friend here ate an apple already, which he didn't mean to only he was overcome at the sight of all the food in your cart and—"

"Think nothing of it. In fact, help yourself to something too. You look as if you could use some nutrition."

"Thanks," Niko said, selecting a plump, juicy pear and biting into it with a sigh of pleasure.

"Well, good luck getting back to your world. The charm should prove most useful."

Niko and Walker looked at each other. "How did you know about the charm?" Walker demanded.

The old man sighed. "I can feel its power radiating from you like a fire. The legend of the nine charms is known in this world, too. Did you know that our worlds used to be one, until the Lords of Time split them apart? Yours was called the First World, ours the Gyre World."

Niko and Walker shook their heads.

"Well, I've been expecting things to start changing ever since the thunderstone fell. It's part of the prophecy, that when the nine charms of the Lords of Time come forth, then will come the changers—the Protector, the Chooser, and the Bearer. And after that, the rising of the dragons—"

The *clip-clop* of hooves on cobblestones echoed in the early-morning quiet.

"Oh, dear. It's my first appointment. I'm afraid you'll have to run along. She would be most distressed if anyone were to see her. After all, she has her reputation to protect, as the daughter of a trader. And no one can know that she has stooped so low as to be involved in magic."

"Magic?" Niko said. "What's that to do with you?"

"I'm a bones reader. A fortune-teller. And no sort of scrying into the future is allowed now that the trader Lyonel Summerwynd has become praefectus regis of the town."

"I don't get it," Walker said. "Fortune-telling isn't magic. There's no such thing as magic."

The old man smiled. "So how did you get here, if it wasn't for magic, young man? Now go, before my appointment arrives."

"I have just one more question," Niko said hesitantly. "What . . . er . . . what happened to that other warrior you mentioned?"

The old man shook his head. "He went north, I believe."

After thanking the old man again, Niko and Walker turned back the way they'd come. They'd only gone a short way when a magnificent horse and carriage came around the corner, forcing them off to the side. Through the window they caught a glimpse of long red hair and deep green eyes, porcelain white skin, and a violet dress. The girl stared at them for a moment, her green eyes lingering on Walker, who Niko noticed had a silly grin on his face.

"Wow!" Walker breathed after the carriage had passed. "She's the most beautiful girl I've ever seen."

"Come on," Niko urged. "You're never going to see her again." Was he ever wrong about that, he'd think over and over again when it was too late to do anything about it.

"Hmm," Walker said absently, turning back to look for the carriage, which had disappeared around the corner.

Leaving the twisting streets behind, Walker and Niko walked back to the harbor boulevard, now bustling with people as the loading and unloading of trading vessels began for the day. The ships were a majestic sight, Niko thought, with their curving prows and rows of silver oarlocks glinting in the sun. Instead of names, each ship bore a different symbol. Niko could see a rose on one tall galley, a lion on another, and a jagged bolt of silver lightning on yet another.

The sight of the ships seemed to bring Walker out of his lovesick trance. "Whoa! Check that out! Looks like the ships in Battle of the Empires, this computer game where——" Walker suddenly whirled around and shouted, "Hey, watch where you're going!"

Niko turned. Beside Walker stood a tall man in a

long, dark, hooded cloak that covered most of his face except for his violet-colored eyes. A cold feeling suddenly gripped Niko, and he shivered.

"Sorry," the man said in a voice that didn't sound sorry at all. "You two looking for work? I could use two more pairs of hands unloading a ship that just docked in the old harbor."

"I don't think——," Niko began.

"The pay is three silvers," the man cut in. "Four if the job is done before sunset."

"Great," Walker said before Niko could contradict him. "We'll do it."

"The old harbor is that way," the stranger said, pointing toward an uneven sidewalk that led away from the harbor to an older section of the city. Then he swept off into the crowd, his dark cloak like a shadow amid the sea of multicolored robes.

"Just think. With three silvers each, we can buy meat and bread and some dessert and something good to drink and . . . ," Walker said as he took off in the direction the stranger had indicated.

"I can't believe you said yes to that man," Niko said, following him. "I have a bad feeling about this."

"Will you stop being so doom and gloom?" Walker countered. "So the dude was a little weird. Big deal. Money is what matters—and food, so quit worrying. Three silvers sounds like big bucks to me."

"I don't know," Niko said, unable to explain his vague misgivings but equally unable to dismiss them as an image of the cloaked man's strange violet eyes hovered uneasily in his mind's eye like some kind of mysterious warning.

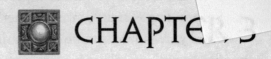 CHAPTER 3

Aurora shivered. The icy wind cut through her thick fur cloak as she climbed higher up the Crystal Claw Mountains. Who'd ever named them had certainly known what they were talking about, she thought. Her feet, warm at first in the fur-lined boots she'd been given days and days ago at Black Rock, felt like blocks of ice now. She put one foot slowly in front of the other, exhausted from so many hours of walking in the bone-chilling cold. Her eyes wandered to the left, to the sheer drop into nothingness. One wrong step and she could go right over the edge. She stumbled suddenly.

"Watch out!" Marcus barked as she fell to her knees in the wet snow. The rope around her waist that tied her to Marcus tightened.

"Keep moving!" a voice shouted from the front.

Aurora tried to get up, but she slipped and fell again, this time bringing Marcus down with her.

"Stupid girl!" Marcus muttered, glaring at her as he struggled to pull himself to his feet. Aurora sighed. She knew Marcus blamed her for the fact that his punishment had been to go on this trip north as her guard. Just then the leader of their group came marching toward them.

Marcus staggered to his feet, head bowed, without saying a word. In the next second, Jah was on him so fast Aurora never even saw him move. He pinned Marcus's arms behind his back and with one finger he pressed a spot on Marcus's neck. The boy instantly turned red and began gasping for air.

"You have much to learn, novice," he said in the flat, monotone voice Aurora had come to hate. "The way of the Dragon requires the mastery of balance."

"Leave him alone!" Aurora shouted. She didn't like Marcus, but she hated Jah more. "It was my fault."

Jah never turned around. He simply let go, allowing Marcus to fall to the ground, and then headed off toward the front of the line of Dragons.

"Sorry," Aurora said, reaching out a hand to help Marcus up.

He brushed her away. "No, you're not. But you're

gonna be, cuz if it wasn't for you, I wouldn't be here at all."

They walked for a long time after that, climbing higher and higher. Aurora began to feel light-headed, her thoughts swimming as images of Niko and her grandmother, Titi, collided with visions of herself and her brother, Kareem, when they were small. Kareem, who was dead to her now. Worse than dead. He had become a Dragon named Jah. She blinked, trying to focus, and she wondered if she was being affected by the magic of the North. People said it got inside your head and drove you crazy.

When the caravan reached a spot so dizzyingly high up that Aurora thought they could go no farther, the procession stopped. No one said a word as they stood clustered at the foot of a sprawling black fortress that seemed hewn of the very rock of the mountain itself.

Aurora blinked the ice from her eyelashes and stared up, dread filling her. Nine Shadows Henge. All she'd picked up about the place from scattered snatches of conversations on their long climb was that Nine Shadows was the heart and soul of the Dragons' power base and at least half of Lord Draco's entire Dragon guard lived and trained here.

"What did you say?" she asked, turning to Marcus.

He stared blankly at her. "Nothin'. I don't got nothin' to say to you."

She heard more whispers in the frigid midnight quiet. Aurora gulped, but she didn't have to look at Marcus to know that he spoke the truth. It was the magic humming through the air. After that she had no more time to think as she passed through the fortress gates into the vast, high-ceilinged entry. In the faint, shadowy light of a few candles she noticed Dragons, lots of them, swords at their hips, lined up along the walls. She also saw that they all wore ear hoops of jacinth—purple stones flecked with gold. Jacinth was a gem known to protect against magic. The only one who wasn't wearing it was Jah. She stared at him, wondering, and as if he had felt her gaze, he turned, looking at her with green eyes that were so like her own that she shivered again.

Without a word he advanced toward her, nodding that she was to precede him. They passed many Dragons along their way through the fortress, until they finally stopped at the top of a steep stairway. Jah removed a key from his cloak and fitted it into the ancient rusting lock. Then he opened the door and pushed her forward into the darkness.

"Sleep well, sister," he murmured in the cold, sneering voice he always used with her. Then the door clanged shut and she heard the rasp of the key in the lock and the muffled thud of footsteps as he left her alone in total darkness.

"I am not your sister," Aurora cried out, tears welling up. She wiped them away impatiently. This was no time to feel sorry for herself. Heart thumping in her chest, she stared into the darkness. She took one tentative step and then another, pushing all worries from her mind about what might be lurking in the room—rats, bats, spiders.

Shifting the heavy fur cloak about her shoulders, Aurora stuck her arms out in front of her and moved forward, feeling her way. Finally her fingers met cold stone. She kept walking, hugging the wall, blinking furiously to adjust her eyes to the darkness, but still she could see nothing. If only she had some light. There was one way, but she didn't know if she could do it. Her powers had been weakened by whatever Lord Draco had done to her mind back at Black Rock, and she was afraid her Gypsy magic might not work. But still she must try. Breathing deeply, she concentrated on the hottest spice she knew, zingiber, white-hot ginger, and tried to summon it into her mind. Her head began to throb painfully and lights floated behind her eyelids. Her body tensed with the effort, but it was no use. Nothing happened.

She sighed and began walking once more. Her fingers trailed listlessly across the stone. Then, suddenly, she felt a gust of cold air. Looking up, she could just make out the faint silvery pinpricks of stars. A window. Without wasting another moment, Aurora jumped. But the ledge was too high to reach. She jumped again and then again, and finally managed to hoist herself up. The moon emerged from behind the clouds just then and she could see why they hadn't bothered putting bars on the window. Far, far below, the mountain peaks glinted sharply in the silver light. Aurora swallowed and looked away as a wave of dizziness washed over her.

Before she could lose her nerve, Aurora climbed through the opening and lowered herself from the sill, her fingers gripping the cold, hard edge. She allowed her body to hang free, forcing herself to focus on the stones in front of her, silvery gray in the moonlight. She was a good climber. She'd climbed the tallest trees in the forest, even ones with trunks so thick and smooth none of the boys had been able to follow. She could scale this wall easily, with all its nooks and crannies. Her toes found a groove in the freezing stone below. The cold bit into her, and her teeth began to chatter as wind swirled ice and snow through the darkness, wetting her cloak and stinging her eyes. The lonely cries of wolves drifted to her from somewhere far away.

Taking a deep breath of frosty air, Aurora moved her freezing fingers, searching for a place to grip. The urge to look down was strong, especially now that she knew there were wolves out there. She found a crevice, then lowered herself gingerly, concentrating so hard that she never heard the near silent flapping of wings. Never saw the great bird swoop down out of the sky, black as night, at one with the darkness. She was almost knocked from her perch.

Aurora cried out from the pain and searched desperately to find a more solid position before the night bird struck again. She'd never make it all the way back to her cell. As the fierce creature circled above her, she moved sideways, grasping edges of jutting stones, hoping for another window, another way in. And finally her fingers found something protruding outward. A ledge. The bird swooped to attack once more, just missing her as she tumbled through a narrow slit in the wall. She landed in a heap, crying out from the pain as her injured hand hit the stone.

"*Shhh!* Or they'll hear you," a voice whispered out of the darkness.

Aurora's breath caught in her throat.

"Who are you?" the voice softly asked.

"Who are *you*?" she countered. She didn't trust anybody or anything in this place, least of all a strange voice in the dark, no matter how innocent it sounded.

"Where did you come from?"

"Why should I tell you?"

"Because you're a prisoner, same as me."

That much was true, Aurora thought. "What is this place?" she asked finally.

"Nine Shadows Henge," the voice answered.

"I know what it's called," Aurora said, "but what's so special about it?" The voice began to speak once more.

"According to tales of the Great Age, Nine Shadows Henge was the burial place of the last great dragons. The white dragon was controlled by the King of the South and the black dragon was controlled by the King of the North. Peace was kept by the Lords of Time, who moved between the worlds and kept the dark and light balanced through their powerful nine charms. Eventually the dragon kings grew greedy and wanted to take control of all the worlds from the Lords of Time. They waged a war for possession of the charms, and after that, according to legend, the kings destroyed each other. The Lords of Time supposedly trapped their dragons in the stones below this place, entombed in the darkness, until the charms would be brought forth once more. Then, according to the prophecy, they would rise and finish the battle their masters began. Since that time there has been no travel between worlds, no connection, no bond and no history."

Aurora took a step closer to the voice, wondering that she'd never heard this story before. There was a soft clap and suddenly the room glowed with dim yellow light, which came from the gleam of amber beads that studded the rough stone walls. Aurora's eyes widened in surprise when she got her first glimpse of the owner of the voice. It was a child. A small boy with curly fair hair, dimples, and tawny yellow eyes. He was six, at most seven. And he was imprisoned in an iron cage just big enough to sit up in. His small white fingers gripped the bars.

"See? You can make light, if you know how to work the magic," the boy said. "This place is riddled with magic. Can you feel it?" Then noticing her bloody hand, he asked, "What happened?"

"A night bird."

The little boy nodded. "I have some verbena. It will help stop the blood."

Aurora's eyebrows rose in surprise.

"They gave it to me," he explained, almost as if he had read her mind. "After the last time they . . ." He gulped, looking away for a moment. "They beat me so badly, I think even they were afraid. Here." He handed her a green spiky leaf.

"Thanks." She reached for it with her good hand, and the boy's eyes widened.

"The Dragon's Eye," he whispered.

Aurora drew back her hand. "What did you say?"

"The sign of the Dragon's Eye. I just saw it on your hand. You're the Protector of the nine charms."

Aurora shook her head. "I don't know what you're talking about," she lied.

"Don't you know me?" the boy urged, his shining eyes golden in the semidarkness.

"No, I don't," she said, but as soon as she spoke she felt a faint tingling in her forehead, a sense of something coming back to her, almost like a memory.

"My name is Kite. I'm the Chooser. That is why I am being held here." His eyes, so young and hopeful, were pleading with her to believe him. "I'm a prisoner of the dark, just like you."

Aurora frowned, thinking that the boy didn't know what he was talking about. Niko was the Chooser.

"Yes, Niko was the Chooser," Kite said.

"You read my mind," Aurora gasped.

"Sorry, I didn't mean to do that," Kite said. "I couldn't help it. Anyway, once Niko left this world, a new Chooser came forth, and that's me. The Dragons know it so they put me in this cage."

Aurora sank to the floor, her thoughts a mad jumble in her brain.

"Don't you see? They've brought you here to cage you up like me so you and I don't find the charms and send one out. Because if we do, they know we'll summon a new Bearer to help us. You have to get the charms, before it's too late. I know the charms are here because the Dragons are planning to use them in some kind of terrible ceremony."

Aurora stared at Kite. Everything suddenly fit into place. Jah's abduction of her and the charms, her conversation with Lord Draco about the charms belonging in this sacred place, being brought here. Still . . .

"Even if you escape and find Niko and the Bearer, you still won't have the charms, will you? How can you leave here without even trying to reclaim them?"

Kite was right. She was the Protector after all.

"But how can I get them?" Aurora burst out. "They're sure to be guarded. Anyway, this room must be locked from the outside, like the cell I was in."

Kite nodded. "Go to the window."

"But the night birds . . ."

"It's not what you think. You don't have to go out the window. Just go over there and count nine stones to your left. Then count nine stones from the floor."

Aurora shrugged and turned toward the window. Maybe the boy really did know something. Either way, she figured she had nothing to lose.

Aurora counted nine stones to the left. Then she counted again, nine stones up. Her fingers touched a large, oblong stone.

"Now push," the boy said.

Aurora leaned all her weight against the stone, but

nothing happened. She pushed harder, grunting with effort. Still nothing.

"Push with your heart," he urged.

Aurora knew what the boy meant, but she hesitated, afraid to even try to use her powers. Afraid of the pain, the dancing lights, the blackness. And of failing.

"Don't be scared," Kite said, so in tune with her thoughts it made her shiver. "You can do it. For you have the magic. You have the power. And no one can take that away from you."

Aurora closed her eyes. The boy was right. She couldn't give up. She inhaled through one nostril and let her breath slowly out through the other, in and out, until she felt the faint tingling in her forehead. There was no pain, no light. Just that telltale surge of power. Aurora's forehead began to burn. She opened her eyes and stared at the stone, commanding it to move, willing it to happen, Kite's words echoing in her mind. You have the magic, you have the power. And suddenly, with a rasping, grating sound, the stone began to move.

"You have the magic. You have the power," Aurora kept repeating as she crept down the dark passageway, using the dim light of an amber bead she had prized from the wall in Kite's cell to find her way. She continued on, down a twisting staircase, the third she'd descended so far. Kite had said everything about Nine Shadows was in multiples of three and remembering that would help her find her way. After the third staircase there would be an entryway and then a pair of huge wooden doors bearing the sign she knew so well. And there it was. The Dragon's Eye. If she hadn't been so excited about her powers and about finding an ally, she might have wondered how Kite knew so much. But she didn't, until much later.

Gently she pushed on the ancient door, but it didn't give. She pushed again, harder. Still it didn't move, but she could hear the wood creaking. Stepping back and ramming her shoulder against it, she was rewarded by the sound of hinges groaning as the door gave way. At the same time, she heard the thud of footsteps right behind her. She swung around, terrified it would be Jah or one of the ferocious Dragon guards. But it was neither—just the boy Marcus.

"What do you think you're doing?" Marcus said, running toward her.

"Leave me alone."

"No." Marcus grabbed her by the arm, and she stared up into his eyes, breathing deeply, feeling the tingle of power rising in her forehead. She pushed past his anger, and before Marcus knew what was happening, she sent a thought into his mind: *Everything is fine. I saw nothing unusual on my watch.*

When she finally tore her eyes away, Marcus released her and turned back down the passage as if nothing had happened. She smiled. She did have the magic and the power. Kite was right.

Aurora proceeded into a dark, eerie space, closing the creaky door behind her. She turned to the right as Kite had directed. Seventy-two steps, he had said. A special number. Eight times nine. She didn't know why—or how he knew—but it would lead her to the charms.

Aurora shivered, counting carefully as she went. The air was icy, almost as if she were outside. Twenty-five, twenty-six, twenty-seven. She saw nothing in front of her. To her left, nothing. To her right, the rough stones of the wall. She continued on, carefully stepping and counting. Fifty-five, fifty-six, fifty-seven. She stopped and stamped her feet, her breath leaving a plume of smoke in the frigid air. On she went. Seventy-one. Seventy-two. And there, straight ahead, was the large stone slab Kite had described. Cast around it were the shadows of nine massive vertical stones, each linked to the one beside it by a stone crosspiece. The nine shadows of Nine Shadows Henge. Beneath the stones, so the story went, the dragons lay buried.

And there, in the center of the ring of stones, lay a

purple velvet pouch. Aurora grabbed it, feeling the hard square shapes within, hearing them clink softly. The charms. At last. Quickly she turned and retraced her steps. She didn't wonder why everything was going so smoothly. The thought never crossed her mind— though it would many times. Later.

Kite was waiting for her when she returned, his eagerness rolling off him in waves.

"Is everything all right?" he asked.

Aurora nodded. "I ran into someone, but he wasn't a problem."

Kite smiled. "Your powers, right? I told you, you have the magic. Now let me see them."

"How do you know I got the charms?"

"I can feel them."

"Here." Aurora thrust the purple pouch through the bars of the cage. "Since you're the Chooser."

"I can't believe it. The nine charms of the Lords of Time."

"Eight," Aurora reminded him.

"Right."

Slowly Kite loosened the tie on the pouch and turned it upside down. The charms spilled out onto the floor of his cage, gleaming with that not-quite-silver, not-quite-gold sheen Aurora remembered. He turned them over one by one so that he could see the luminous gemstones, the rich green and blue and purple and yellow like a rainbow in the dark room. They both stared at the charms in awed silence.

"I'm going to choose one," Kite whispered finally. "And then I'll give it to you to send out."

Aurora nodded, feeling strangely light-headed, almost as if she were in a dream. She worried that she'd never be able to do what she had done with the red charm.

"Don't doubt yourself," Kite reassured her.

She watched as he closed his eyes and began to breathe deeply. His fingers played over the charms as his breathing quickened. When he opened his eyes, they had a faraway look, focused on something only he could see. His tiny, little-boy fingers finally stopped on the charm with a pale blue stone in its center, a blue like the morning sky.

"This is the one."

Carefully he handed it to her. The charm felt warm, as if it were a living thing. Aurora closed her eyes and began to chant as she had on that night so long ago with Niko. She let the words flow through her as they had then, not thinking of anything, just letting the music take her, the Old Ones' chant of joy and sorrow, of the endless transformation of life, of what was and what would be. The ancient words rolled off her tongue into the silent room, where in the cadence of her voice echoed the voices of the old ones. The charm grew hotter. She tried to hold on for as long as she could, but it was too hot. She dropped it with a cry. But instead of the clink of metal on stone, there was only silence.

Slowly Aurora opened her eyes and blinked.

"The black dragon will rise," Kite hissed in a strange new voice, much deeper than the sweet, high voice she'd heard before.

Aurora stared in horror at the boy, whose face suddenly looked old beyond its years. What had she done? she wondered in a panic. But it was too late.

The blue charm had been sent out, and no matter how much she might want to, there was no bringing it back.

CHAPTER 4

Niko and Walker approached the majestic wooden ship at the dock, its paint fresh, its planks scrubbed and oiled, its sails crisp and white. Most striking of all was the single white flower with long, drooping petals painted on one side of the ship. They could see men already hard at work, unloading crates from the hold below, stacking, sorting, and arranging them on the dock. The boys were near enough to catch fragments of conversation.

". . . coming of the dragon. That's what that thunderstone means, falling like it done from a burnin' sky," said a pale thin man with a whiny voice.

At the words "dragon" and "thunderstone" the boys looked at each other.

"Burnin' sky?" guffawed a tall man as he heaved a crate off his shoulders and banged it onto the dock.

"Burnin' cuz we ain't had no rain in so long is what. And then that thing fallin' from the sky. It's a sign for sure," the first man continued. "A bad omen."

The tall man laughed. "You hear that, mates? Jek here thinks the black dragon is gonna rise and start shootin' fire out of its bleedin' mouth and bring on the end of the world, sizzlin' us all up like some cook fire gone out of control. Ain't that how that superstitious mumbo jumbo goes?"

"I'm tellin' you," insisted the man called Jek. "The end is comin'. Unless the white dragon is waked to fight the black, then we're all gonna die. Burn up like moths in a flame."

"You're burnin' me up all right," said a stoop-shouldered man dressed in drab brown cotton with drab brown hair to match as he descended the plank to the dock. "Now let's go, lackeys. If you don't get back to work, I'll make that one silver piece instead of three. Or none at all if you don't please me."

Niko noticed that the man was wearing a long gold chain with a glittering purple medallion flecked with yellow. Jacinth. Niko remembered from his mineral studies with Lord Amber that jacinth could guard against magic, or so some believed.

"What are you lookin' at, boy?" the steward barked.

"Nothing," Niko said.

"We're here to work," Walker added.

"You two will be runners. You run the stuff from the hold up to the deck and then hustle back down. If you're fast enough and don't break nothin' then you'll get your money, but only if. Now go."

The steward practically pushed them down the steps to the hold. They found Jek and his mates in a large, low-ceilinged space filled with crates of varying shapes and sizes, along with planks of rough-cut timber that smelled like cedar.

"Wow!" Walker burst out, staring around the hold. "Whose stuff is all this?"

"Lyonel Summerwynd's," the tall man answered. "It's the first shipment from the Forbidden Isles. The best amber, ivory, timber, and furs anybody's ever seen."

Summerwynd, Niko thought, as he picked up one of the crates, straining from the weight. The bones reader had told them that the praefectus of the town was named Summerwynd.

"Pretty heavy, huh?" Walker panted as he turned to climb the steps to the deck. "But just think about the food we'll eat when we're done and that'll make it all worth it, right?"

Niko didn't answer, unable to shake his feelings of

foreboding as he shouldered his crate and struggled up the stairs. After that, however, he had no more time to think. Down and up the two boys went for what felt like hours, until they both collapsed onto the deck to catch their breath.

"This is like slave labor," Walker muttered. "I mean, working this hard in the hot sun with nothing to drink. It's not right. We should organize, start a picket line—"

"Get a move on!" the steward shouted, rushing around the deck, his face as red as the bald spot on his head. "Get up and straighten those crates. Hurry it up. Let's go."

"What's with the steward?" Walker asked as Jek slipped quietly beside them.

"See over there," he said. Jek pointed toward the end of the waterway that led from the harbor. A sleek pleasure boat was skimming toward them, moving dangerously fast, paying no heed to the other traffic. Niko watched as barges and skiffs moved aside to clear a path.

"I don't get it," Walker said. "Doesn't that little boat have to give way to the traffic, not the other way around?"

"Not if Lyonel Summerwynd's on it," Jek said.

"You over there!" the steward shouted at Niko and Walker. "Get ready to hoist that plank for the praefectus regis."

Niko and Walker lifted the polished wooden plank and watched as the pleasure boat drew up alongside. The steward motioned for other crew members to grab the ropes from the smaller ship and secure them.

Minutes later Walker and Niko watched a tall, well-muscled man with a shock of steel gray hair mount their ship.

"Your presence does us a great honor, Praefectus," the steward murmured, bowing his head.

Lyonel Summerwynd nodded curtly, his eyes scanning the deck as if he was looking for someone. "Has the trader Ikbar arrived?"

"He's down below, Praefectus," the steward answered in a tight voice, nervously fingering his pendant. "He says he is inspecting the cargo from the North."

Niko noticed that the steward emphasized the word "says," as if he didn't really believe this Ikbar.

"Father, will you be long?" called a girl's voice from the pleasure boat. Niko craned his neck to see who had spoken. Standing on the prow of the sleek craft beneath a striped awning of purple and white was a girl in a lilac dress. She had long red hair and sparkling green eyes.

"I will gladly wait for—"

"Nonsense, Elyana," Lyonel Summerwynd boomed. "You run along. I'll see you at home later."

"It's her," Walker whispered, staring at the girl on

the boat. "Niko, it's the girl from the carriage, the one from this morning."

Niko nodded, realizing that this girl must be the praefectus's daughter, which meant that she had broken her own father's rule about not dabbling in magic. But he didn't say anything to Walker, who was staring at Elyana with a silly grin on his face.

"Dream on, kid," muttered one of Jek's mates, prodding Walker in the back. "Let's go, boys." With that he half pushed them back down the stairs.

"Elyana is beautiful, isn't she?" Jek whispered as they got on with their work. "Her mother was from the South like me. From the Vale of Leaves. You can tell by the red hair."

After that they had no more time to talk as the steward forced them on at a grueling pace. Just when Niko thought he would faint if he didn't get some water and a moment's rest, the steward called a break. Most of the crew grabbed a final crate and hurried up on deck. Walker, Niko, and Jek were left in the hold. Sighing, they wiped their sweaty faces with their shirts. Just as they were about to head up, they heard a door clanging open, followed by footsteps clattering across the hold. In the murky half-light Niko could make out who it was.

Lyonel Summerwynd stared past Niko, Walker, and Jek as if they weren't there, a self-satisfied smile on his face as he took in the crates and cedar planks. "Truly one of the finest cargoes I've ever seen," he said, looking back into the shadows.

"Thank you, Praefectus," murmured a voice that prickled the hairs on Niko's neck. Into the light stepped a dark, hooded figure—the man with the violet eyes.

"Ikbar, I can see I made a very wise decision when I chose to do business with you. Your contacts in the North have served me well," Lyonel Summerwynd purred. "From a professional as well as a personal point of view I could not be happier. Not only have I found a new route to the North, but through you I've also found the perfect fiancé for my daughter."

Both men laughed as if they shared some sort of joke and then disappeared into one of the aft cabins.

"What was he talking about?" Walker asked. "Is Elyana getting married?"

"Dunno, boy," Jek said in his nasal voice.

"Come on," Niko said. "We'd better get a move on or there won't be any water left for us."

Walker nodded and bent for a crate just as Niko did, but in their exhaustion they grabbed the same one. Walker decided to let Niko have it at the same moment that Niko decided it was Walker's. As they both let go, the crate thudded to the floor. The lid popped off and dark, fishy-smelling furs spilled out like black puddles onto the wood floor.

Niko and Walker glanced up the ladder. Apparently no one had heard the noise.

"Quick! Let's get that stuff back in there!" Walker urged.

They bent over the crate and began to shove the oily furs inside.

"Hurry," Walker said. "I bet the break's almost over."

He and Niko had patted the lid of the crate back into place when they noticed Jek standing there. With a look of terror he was staring at something on the floor behind them.

"Jek, what's the matter?" Niko asked.

Jek didn't answer but he pointed to a small green bottle. Niko figured it must have rolled out of the crate when he and Walker dropped it.

Walker moved to pick it up.

"Watch out!" Jek hissed, coming out of his trance.

"What are you talking about? It's just a bottle and I need to put it back where it belongs before the steward comes down and kills us."

"It's dream water," Jek murmured, his eyes riveted on the little green bottle. "Dark magic."

"Well, whatever it is, I'm just going to put it back where it belongs," Walker said.

"Wait!" Niko said, his gaze shifting from the bottle to Walker. "I mean, I've heard of dream water too.

When I studied the culture of the Cold Edge, of the far reaches of the North. People there were known as the dream makers, and they used the water for different purposes. I think it's supposed to bring visions."

"So?" Walker said.

"So I think we should be careful with it, that's all. I mean, you don't know how it might affect you."

Walker shook his head at Niko, a half smile on his face. "You kill me, you know that? Here you are this warrior guy who can bring down a roomful of bigger kids, but you're afraid of some green water."

With that, Walker bent and picked up the bottle, pausing to study it for a moment.

"Put it away now," Jek implored, his palms together as if he were praying. "Hurry, boy."

"Come on, Walker," Niko said, moving closer.

But Walker was staring at the bottle as if transfixed. And Niko saw that dripping down its side was one droplet of clear liquid that shimmered with rainbow lights. He watched as Walker reached one finger toward it.

"Don't!" Niko cried, throwing himself on Walker. He grabbed the bottle and the droplet of dream water dripped onto his finger. A sweet, spicy smell pierced his nostrils.

"Get it away!" Jek whined, but Niko barely heard him. The smell was familiar, but he couldn't think why.

Reminded him of something . . . He couldn't remember. Suddenly the room began to spin. He took a deep breath, but that only seemed to make things worse. Everything got blurry—the outlines of the crates, Walker beside him, Jek's silhouette. He blinked, trying to focus.

He heard a familiar cak-caking and Topaz, his pet falcon, swooped toward him, her yellow eyes gleaming. The bird perched on his shoulder and cawed again as a rasping voice said, "Come here, boy. Let us play another round of White Elephant."

It was the master, Lord Amber, and he was sitting in front of the fire in the great hall of the Castle of the Seven Towers, the tiles of the game scattered on a table before him.

The housekeeper, Ruah, was there too, holding out a plate of sweet cakes.

"Come, Niko, you look hungry, boy," she said in her lilting accent.

Niko smiled at his old friends as Topaz gently pecked his ear.

Wait a minute, he thought. This isn't real. Lord Amber is dead and so is Ruah. And Topaz is gone.

Niko sighed, wishing his vision were real—

Rough hands snatched the bottle from Niko's fingers. He fell to the floor, flashes of his vision still lingering. Crates crashed to the floor around him, and he thought he heard a scream.

Niko tried to stand, but his legs were wobbly. He felt himself pushed backward into the wall of crates. His head hit the wood painfully, knocking the last of the dream vision out of his mind. That was when Niko saw the blood. It was everywhere, spilling onto the wooden floor, pooling at his feet. Lying in the blood was Jek, his fingers still clutching the bottle that had started it all.

"Jek," Niko murmured. He shook the man's shoulder, but Jek didn't move.

"He's dead," a voice snarled.

Startled, Niko turned to see a hooded figure. Ikbar. The man with the violet eyes was holding a bloodied knife and glaring down at Niko.

"Why did you kill him?" Niko blurted out.

"The same reason that I'm going to kill you—for seeing something that was not meant for your eyes."

Ikbar raised the knife to strike when Niko caught movement out of the corner of his eye. Walker threw himself on the trader, who managed to shake him off as if he were swatting a fly. But in the process Ikbar dropped his knife. Niko jumped to his feet as Walker lunged for the knife and managed to kick Ikbar hard in one shin. The trader groaned but didn't fall, and advanced toward Niko with a menacing glare.

"Watch out, Niko!" Walker cried, bounding across the hold clutching the bloody knife.

Before he could again hurl himself on the cloaked

man, Walker's pants caught on the edge of one of the crates. As he jerked away, his pocket ripped, and the red charm fell to the floor. Niko and Walker both were lunging to retrieve it when Ikbar turned and hit Niko hard in the back. As Niko went down groaning, he saw the man beat Walker to the charm and pocket it with a surprised smile, as if he realized exactly what he'd just found.

"Hey," Walker protested, advancing toward Ikbar, still holding the knife.

"Give that back," Niko demanded, bolder now that Ikbar was distracted by their treasure. The boy scrambled to his feet and jumped on the cloaked man, pummeling him with his fists while Walker circled with the knife. But the trader barely reacted. He just pushed Niko off with one quick shove, then opened his mouth in mock horror.

"Murderer!" he cried, pointing at Walker, his voice booming loud enough for everyone else on board to hear.

Within seconds pounding feet dashed toward the hold. Walker dropped the knife with a clatter. Then he and Niko tore up the steps. They couldn't stop to get the charm back now. No one would believe their story, Niko knew. Not two poor kids in raggedy tunics, one stained with blood. Not when it would be their word against a trader's. By the time they reached the top of the steps, the steward and two burly shiphands were bearing down on them. The two boys crouched by the door of the hold, looking around in panic.

"Stop the murderer!" the steward cried, seeing Walker's bloody clothes.

Niko glanced around frantically. They had only one option. Walker must have been thinking the same thing. Before Niko could say a word, Walker had leaped for the ship's railing. Niko bounded after Walker.

"Get them!" the steward yelled.

But the boys had jumped off the side of the ship into the water below.

CHAPTER 5

Zoe had to be dreaming. There was no other explanation for the hot sun beating down from the cloudless blue sky or the strange stone jars that lay scattered around her or the dusty mountain road that led to some kind of seaside town with pastel-colored houses.

Feeling like Alice lost in Wonderland, she walked over to one of the jars and touched its cracked surface. There was writing on it, but it didn't say "Drink me" or "Eat me." As she picked it up to look more closely, it slipped out of her fingers and shattered. Inside was some sort of powder . . . or ashes. Zoe shivered. She didn't like this place, this dream.

"Wake up!" she ordered herself. "Wake up!"

But when she opened her eyes, she saw in panic that the stone shards were still scattered over the rocky ground. She was still here, wherever here was. The last thing she could remember was being caught outside with a storm coming and then . . . nothing. She struggled to remember, pacing around the jars without seeing them anymore, ignoring the huge black boulder that blocked the path down the mountain just yards away. What was she not remembering? At least she had her wallet—she could feel its bulky outline in her pocket. She would use her mother's credit card to call her father and tell him to come get her. But when she stuck her hand into her pocket, she felt a cold, hard shape nestled beside her wallet. Slowly she pulled it out. The blue stone gleamed in the sun with its cool light.

Zoe stroked the gem's smooth surface as everything came flooding back. She bit her lip and tried not to cry. She remembered finding this charm by the pond, then the lightning and falling in the shallow water. And now, presto, she was here.

"Where am I?" Zoe wondered aloud, taking a deep breath and trying to calm down.

"Tyrosss, one of the most important ssseaports in the Gyre World," a soft voice hissed. "A city of traders through which goods from all four corners pass on their journeys north, sssouth, eassst, and wessst."

Zoe whirled around, but no one was there. Just a lizard sunning itself on a rock.

"Don't look so surprised. You know something momentousss has happened to you."

Zoe glanced around, her heart thumping in her chest. But still there was no one.

"Where are you?" she gasped.

"Where are you?" echoed the voice, and Zoe heard a faint tinkling like wind chimes that almost sounded like laughter.

"I'm not interested in playing some stupid little game, whoever you are. I have money and a credit card, so if you'll just tell me where the nearest phone is, I'll call my dad and he'll come get me. I'll pay you, if you want. Just tell me where I can find a phone."

Zoe heard the same tinkling. There was a pause.

"There are no telephones here."

"What are you talking about? There are phones everywhere."

"Lissssten to me carefully, Zoe. There are no phones here. There are no cars, either. Or computers. There are no movies or soccer games or shopping malls. Thisss is not your world."

"My world?"

"Yesss, your world. Earth, as you have been taught to call it. Thisss is the Gyre World, which was once joined with the Firssst World, from which came the nine charms of the Lords of Time, one of which you now hold in your hand."

Zoe gulped, staring down at the silvery gold square.

"You are the Bearer of the blue charm, and as sssuch you must accomplish certain tasks before you can return home."

"Listen, I don't know who you are or where you are or what kind of sick joke you think you're playing, but if you think I'm going to stand here for one more minute talking about different worlds like I'm trapped in some stupid episode of *Star Trek*, you've got another—"

With a *whoosh* like the soft play of wind through leaves, Zoe watched in shock as four glowing green forms took shape before her, floating like ghosts in a horror movie. But these were four beautiful women—actually three women and one girl about Zoe's age—in flowing blue green dresses that sparkled as if flecked with sequins. Their long, golden hair was woven with feathers, and their blue eyes glittered like sapphires. They hovered before her, part spirit, part flesh, gazing hungrily at what Zoe held in her hand. She stared at them speechlessly, her fingers unconsciously gripping the charm more tightly.

"I am Ijada, the Grand High, eldest Sister of the Kuxan-Sunn, guardians of the pathways between the worlds," the middle one announced. Zoe could see on closer inspection that the creature had a few wrinkles and some white in her hair. "Though we did not choose you, you have been chosen. We have come to help you."

"Help me what?" Zoe burst out.

"Accomplish the task of the second Bearer."

"Huh?"

"You have been sssummoned by the Chooser and the Protector of the nine charms. They sent out that charm and it called you forth."

"Called me to do what? And why me?"

Ijada didn't answer. She looked to the other Sisters before turning back to Zoe.

"Listen, I don't know what this mumbo jumbo is about. But I'm not interested. All I want is to go home."

The Sisters laughed then, the same tinkling sound Zoe had heard earlier.

"It's not funny, you know."

"No, it is not," Ijada agreed, her blue eyes locked on Zoe's. "It is very, very serious. And there is not much time. Listen to me and listen carefully. If you do not do as I sssay, you will never return home. That much is the truth. So lisssten well."

Zoe's eyes moved from Ijada to the youngest Sister, who smiled as if the two of them shared a secret.

"Okay. So what do you want me to do?" Zoe finally said.

"It is not what I want," Ijada insisted, floating so close to Zoe that the girl could see the glittering gems woven into her flowing golden hair. "It is what must be done."

"Whatever. Just tell me. And if it's . . . if it's okay, then I'll do it, I guess. . . ." Zoe figured saying that much didn't really commit her. Anyway, what did it matter if she lied to these wackos? They weren't even human as far as she could tell. They were giving her the creeps and she wanted them to leave her alone.

"You must get the red charm, the charm of fire and blood, from Walker, the first Bearer. But you cannot simply take it; he must give it to you willingly."

"Who's Walker?"

"He is a boy from your world."

"Yeah, okay, so how will I know him?"

Ijada nodded to the littlest Sister, who closed her eyes and circled her arms in the air before her. "Concentrate, Mynerva," Ijada ordered.

The girl moved her hands furiously, over and over making concentric circles, her brow furrowed, and when she opened her eyes again, Zoe could see a boy standing in the space where her hands had been. He had short blond hair and a dirty face, and he was wet, as if he'd been swimming. He was sort of cute in a boyish kind of way.

"Uh . . . hi," Zoe said.

But the boy just stared past her.

"He can't hear you," Ijada explained. "Or sssee you

for that matter. He is an apparition, a vision, conjured up for the sole purpossse of viewing."

Zoe's eyes widened. "How did you do that?"

"It is one of our many ssskills." She turned to Mynerva. "Thank you, Mynerva."

With a few more hand motions from the young one, the image of Walker shredded apart like a Roman candle on the Fourth of July, wisps hanging in the air before vanishing completely.

"Wow!" Zoe said before she could stop herself. Then she turned back to Ijada. "So what now?"

"You cannot sssimply appear in Tyros as you are without arousing suspicion. So you will be posing as Zecropia Palmata, who has come from the Sssouth to visit her cousin, Elyana Summerwynd, and lend much needed female sssupport. Mistress Summerwynd is long dead, so you will not be closely supervised. Of course, the cousins have never met before."

"Back up a minute," Zoe said, frowning. "Why does Elyana need my support?"

"Because she has jussst been told by her father, the illustrious Lyonel Summerwynd, trader *extraordinaire* and praefectus regis of Tyros, that he has promised her hand in marriage to a very powerful lord from far acrosss the sea. Actually, the sea is not really accurate, as this lord is from a place much farther away than that, but be that as it may, Elyana is in bit of a turmoil. She is supposed to meet her new fiancé any day now but she has told her father she refuses to marry someone she's never met."

"So what am I supposed to do?"

"You are supposed to convince her that she mussst marry this lord."

"Me?"

Ijada and the other Sisters nodded.

"How am I supposed to do that?"

Ijada shrugged as a shimmer ran through her blue green dress and ruffled her golden hair.

"That is up to you."

"What if I can't do it?"

Ijada's eyes darkened and her beautiful face turned hard and menacing. A shiver ran up and down Zoe's spine despite the heat of the sun.

"That is not an option. You will convince Elyana that she mussst marry Lord Draco."

"Okay, so suppose I do that, how does that kid Walker figure in all this? How am I supposed to find him?"

"He will find you. Or rather, events will consssspire to throw the two of you together—the prophecy is not explicit about such minor details—at which point you will get his charm. Be warned, however. The Bearer of the charm of fire and blood is a great deal more cunning than he looks. But for one with your keen intelligence and manipulative powers successs is possible."

A warm feeling filled Zoe at the Grand High Sister's compliments. These ghost women were pretty cool, she decided. "How do you know events will bring us together?"

"Ssso many questions. We Sisters can sssee the future, that is how."

"Then you know what is going to—"

Ijada put her fingers to her lips. "*Shhh!* That is all you need to know."

"So if I convince Elyana to marry this Draco guy and I get the red charm from Walker, then I can go home."

Ijada nodded. "You will need the appropriate attire for your visit."

Ijada turned to the other three Sisters, who began to hum, and a steamer trunk appeared with the words Zecropia Palmata, Vale of Leaves, engraved on the top in gold. Out of the trunk Ijada extracted a beautiful pale pink silk sheath and matching pants encrusted with gems and woven with golden thread. It looked like something an Indian princess would wear.

"It's beautiful," Zoe gushed. "Are those diamonds?"

Ijada nodded. "And sapphires and rubies and pearls. Now get dressed." She handed over the clothes. "We'll escort you to the Summerwynd estate to meet your long-losssst cousin."

Zoe fingered the silk, marveling at the way the gemstones glittered in the sunlight. Imagine owning clothes like these, she thought in amazement. For a moment, she wondered where the real Zecropia Palmata was. She was about to ask the Sisters what had happened to her but decided it might be better not to know.

CHAPTER 6

Zoe kicked the cream-colored silk sheets to the foot of the bed and pulled aside the mosquito netting. Moonlight bathed the room in silver as she sat up and fanned herself with the jade-and-ruby-encrusted fan Elyana had so casually tossed to her before bedtime. It looked like something out of a museum. It had to be worth hundreds of thousands, maybe millions, but Elyana had acted as if it were nothing. She moved her arm up and down fast, hoping to cool herself, but it didn't help. Even at night the heat in Tyros was unbearable. Forget air conditioners. These people didn't even know there was such a thing as electricity. They'd never heard of Benjamin Franklin and his stupid kite that got hit by lightning, or whatever.

Sighing, she pulled the ivory-handled cord next to

the bed. Faintly a small bell tinkled somewhere deep in the house. Zoe smiled. In minutes she could hear the patter of footsteps on the marble floor of the hall, then her bedroom door swung open to reveal a gray-haired maid dressed in a plain blue robe. The woman approached the bed and bowed.

"Sela, I want another glass of lemon water," Zoe ordered with an imperious toss of her head, "with sugar . . . I mean *sukkar.*"

"Yes, Miss Zecropia," the servant murmured, bowing once more before she scurried out of the room.

"And make sure the water is really cold this time," Zoe called after her.

She smiled. Although she'd only been at the Summerwynds' for a few days, she had to admit that except for the heat, Tyros wasn't such a bad place. Golden bathtubs the size of swimming pools, a personal servant at your beck and call. It didn't get much better than that. "And what about a few of those honeycakes," she added as an afterthought, glancing toward the door and seeing that Sela was gone.

"Stupid woman," Zoe muttered. "She didn't even wait for me to finish."

She slipped into the jeweled slippers by the side of the bed and headed for the hallway, looking toward the left in the direction of the kitchen and dining rooms. It was late and the hallway was dark and quiet. Sela was nowhere in sight. This meant Zoe could either walk all the way to the kitchen herself or wait for the maid to come back, then send her off again. Definitely the latter. She was just turning back to enter her room again when she sensed a movement behind her. Out of the corner of her eye she noticed a shadow not far from the double doors that led to Elyana's room. Zoe froze. Maybe those strange half-human creatures of the Kuxan whatever-it-was had come to spy on her.

Just act naturally, she told herself as she turned and headed down the hallway. Instead of moving toward the kitchen, she hid herself in one of the marble alcoves. Crouching in the darkness, she waited. After a few tense minutes she heard the sound of approaching footsteps. Zoe leaned forward a bit and caught a glimpse of a cloaked figure, which chose just that moment to turn. Zoe saw the unmistakable glint of red hair.

Elyana! Zoe thought in surprise. What was she doing sneaking around her own house in the middle of the night?

Elyana moved toward the door that led to the courtyard and disappeared. Curious, Zoe followed her. Gently she pushed on the ornate mahogany door. She scanned the courtyard, but Elyana, if it really was

Elyana, was not there. Zoe took a few steps more, squinting into the darkness, but still she saw no one. Disappointed, she turned and reached for the door. Suddenly she felt someone clutch her hand. The scream froze in her throat.

"Cousin," Elyana whispered.

"Oh, Elyana," Zoe blurted out. "You startled me."

"Why are you following me?"

"I . . . uh . . . I wasn't following you, I was just getting some air. It's so hot."

Elyana nodded and smiled gently. "Well, I must go. I have to see someone."

"In the middle of the night? Can't it wait till morning?"

Elyana shook her head, her green eyes fixed on Zoe. "You've got to promise me you won't tell Father."

"Are you in some kind of trouble?"

Elyana bit her lip and looked away. "I don't know. That's why I have to go. I had this strange dream about a white dragon, and I have to find out. . . ." Her voice trailed off. "I must go now. I'll see you in the morning."

"Why don't I go with you?" Zoe suggested as an idea popped into her mind. "I'll keep you company so you're not all alone in the dark."

Elyana pursed her lips, thinking. "All right, if you wish. But dabbling in magic is forbidden, you know."

"That's okay," Zoe said, barely paying attention, all her thoughts on the major blackmail opportunity.

Elyana led them to the stables, where she handed Zoe the groom's coat to put on over her nightgown. She opened a stall and brought out a beautiful white horse, an Arabian, Zoe thought, the kind of horse that sappy Megan liked so much. Elyana gracefully slipped her foot in the stirrups and mounted the horse. She leaned down to pull Zoe up behind her.

"Go, Moonlight!" she said.

The horse cantered out of the stable and through the estate's gates.

"Who do you have to see?" Zoe asked, leaning forward, her hair blowing back in the wind.

"A bones reader," Elyana answered.

"A what?"

"Bones reader. I need to find out what my dream means. He can scry."

"Scry?"

"See the future."

Bones. Scry. Whatever. This place was so so weird, Zoe couldn't wait to get home. Although on second thought, maybe this . . . reader . . . could tell her whether she and Shane Landers would ever go out on a real date.

The two girls rode into the heart of the ancient city.

As the streets narrowed, Elyana urged the horse through the deserted alleyways. Finally, they stopped at a run-down corner.

"Are we there?" Zoe asked in surprise.

"We're close," Elyana answered, sounding distracted as she scanned the area. "It's right around the corner, but that's strange. . . ."

"What?" Zoe asked, craning her neck to see what Elyana meant. Just visible in the moonlight on the opposite side of the alley, the wooden door of the only well-kept house in the entire seedy neighborhood had been flung open.

"Something is wrong," Elyana whispered as she dismounted.

Zoe stared from the door to Elyana. She didn't normally believe in hunches, but she had a bad feeling about this place. "Why don't we come back tomorrow?" she suggested from her perch on the horse.

But Elyana wasn't listening. Carefully she made her way to the other side of the alley, and with her back to the wall she slowly began to edge closer to the door. The girl was impossible, Zoe thought. Sometimes she was so sappy sweet and innocent it made her blood curdle, and the next minute she was acting like an FBI Special Forces agent or something.

Zoe, who had never been much of a horseback rider, slid down the horse's side and nearly sprained her ankle when she hit the ground. Righting herself, she ran across the alleyway, following the path Elyana had taken. She watched as Elyana slid through the open doorway without even a backward glance. Zoe shook her head and followed.

Both girls stood in the cramped stone entranceway, peering into the darkness. There was a small passage out to a garden and a flight of crooked stone steps that led to an upper story. Elyana moved toward the steps when a crash from above was followed by the thud of footsteps and bloodcurdling screams.

"Let's get out of here," Zoe whispered, her heart in her throat. But Elyana had already begun to make her way up the steps.

Zoe followed reluctantly, wishing that she hadn't come at all. It was one thing to try and fulfill her crazy mission, but she wasn't about to die doing it. Still, it was too late for that, she reasoned, and joined her "cousin" on the small landing that overlooked the entrance. Elyana moved toward a closed door and slowly eased it open. The room was in chaos. Books and charts littered the floor, along with a bunch of dusty white sticks of various sizes. Probably the fortune-telling bones, Zoe figured. A cloying sweet and spicy smell hung in the air. Suddenly, the banging started again. It was coming from behind the only other door in the room. Elyana moved toward it, her expression grim and determined.

"I don't think this is such a good idea," Zoe whispered, grabbing Elyana's arm. "We should go get help."

Elyana's green eyes blazed and she shook Zoe off. The banging grew louder. Zoe cringed, staring at the door and putting one foot slowly in front of the other as she followed Elyana. Neither of them noticed the shadow that was creeping behind an overturned bookcase near the far wall. Elyana stood before the door and Zoe held her breath as she watched her reach for the crude latch. With one quick motion Elyana flung open the door.

Zoe stared in horror, swallowing vigorously a few times so she wouldn't throw up. Inside was an old man bound to a chair. There was a gag in his mouth and blood running down the side of his head, matting the long silver hair that framed his wrinkled face. But worst of all were his piercing blue eyes, wide open and staring, the pupils huge and black, filled with fear and something even more terrible—insanity.

"No!" Elyana exclaimed, her hand to her mouth. "It's Taschen, the bones reader."

She reached for the gag and tried to pull it out of the old man's mouth, but it was tied with some kind of trick knot and wouldn't loosen. In her panic Elyana began to pull on the rope that bound Taschen to the chair, but it was no use.

"We need a knife," Elyana burst out as she continued to yank on the rope.

Zoe stared wildly around the room.

"Just find something sharp!" Elyana shouted. "Hurry!"

Zoe ran toward the overturned table in the center of the room, cursing herself for coming on this little late-night expedition. The sight of the old man made her feel so sick it was all she could do not to hurl. Luckily, at that moment she spotted something on the floor. A knife. She reached for it and was just about to turn when she noticed the shadowy figure behind the bookcase. Zoe's mouth went dry. Whoever had done this to the old man was obviously still in the room.

Gripping the knife, she ran back across the room and handed it to Elyana.

"There's someone else here," Zoe whispered in a panicked voice.

But Elyana appeared not to hear her. She cut the gag and pulled it out of the old man's mouth. Strings of saliva and blood hung from it, making Zoe's queasy stomach flip-flop again.

"Taschen," Elyana murmured tenderly, holding the old man's face gently in her hands. How could she touch that senile creature? Zoe wondered. But Taschen did not look at Elyana. His crazy eyes were fixed on Zoe.

"We have to get out of here," Zoe urged Elyana as Taschen suddenly spoke in a harsh, gasping voice.

"Why does the one of the light doubt herself? She has been tricked by the dark, just as I was tricked. Yes, the dark is master of deceit."

His words sent a chill up Zoe's spine, but Elyana seemed not to have heard. She dropped the dagger and was wiping the old man's bleeding head with a strip of fabric she had torn from her dress.

"Don't talk anymore, Taschen," she pleaded, her eyes full of tears. "Save your strength."

"Elyana," Zoe hissed, her voice rising in panic. "I'm telling you, there's someone else in the room."

Elyana's eyes locked on Zoe's. "Zoe, just cut him loose, please, while I try to stop the blood."

"*I* was the one who betrayed the light," Taschen continued in the same crazy voice. "I was the one who was used by the dark, by the Dragon warrior who convinced me to lead the warrior of the silver sword to the other place. Then the door closed and the Dragon warrior was gone and the one with the silver sword was trapped here with no way home. I was the one who betrayed the warrior of the silver sword and Lord Amber. . . ."

Zoe stared, transfixed by the contorted features and wildly rolling eyes of the madman. At that moment there came a crashing sound from across the room and a figure darted out from behind the bookcase. Both girls turned to see a boy with dirty brown hair and a blue tunic staring desperately at Taschen.

"Lord Amber?" the boy cried. "What do you know of Lord Amber?"

"No, Niko, don't!" shouted another voice, as a second boy emerged from the shadows. Zoe's mouth dropped open. It was the boy named Walker.

"How cunning the dark is, posing as the light," the old man ranted. "Those who appear good so often are those of the dark, and those who appear dark are really of the light. . . ."

"What is he talking about?" Walker asked, moving next to Elyana.

"Who did this to you?" Elyana implored the old man.

"We did," Walker said simply. "I had to use the trick knots I learned in camp because he kept breaking loose."

"Someone gave him dream water," Niko explained. "So he's crazy with visions. Whoever it was must have wanted to kill him—they gave him a whole bottle."

Walker frowned then as if he had just thought of something. "Don't you think it's strange that someone tried to kill him with dream water? I mean, there are definitely easier ways to kill someone. Remember our last encounter with dream water? Someone was killed then, too."

Niko stared at Walker. "You mean by Ikbar? But why would he want to kill a bones reader, and why with dream water?"

"I don't know. Maybe it's a terrible way to die. It sure seems as if—"

"I'll tell you why they want me dead. Only I can stand in the way of the dark and prevent the joining of the black and white dragons, the joining prophesied to bring about the end of all the worlds. The Dark Sorcerer sent one of his emissaries to stop me; it was the man with the violet eyes, a Skyggni. For only I can tell the white dragon queen of her true destiny, of the prophecy of the light." The old man paused, then turned his eyes to Elyana and then Zoe.

"I know who you really are," Taschen burst out, his eyes blazing with sudden clarity. "And you will not succeed. You will not surrender the white dragon to the power of the black—"

"He's delirious," Zoe said. "Out of his mind. Totally nuts." But her voice shook a little. Why did this old man think he knew anything about her? Unless maybe he really could scry, or whatever Elyana had said meant looking into the future.

"The dark is come," intoned the old man, his still, clear eyes never leaving Zoe's face.

"We can't leave him like this," Elyana said, and before the others could stop her, she picked up the knife and began to cut the ropes.

"I wouldn't do that," Walker said.

"We can't keep him tied like a prisoner," Elyana countered as the ropes fell away and Taschen was released.

"I will not allow the dark to betray the light again," Taschen shouted, staggering toward the center of the room.

"Stop him!" Elyana cried.

Niko and Walker both ran toward the old man, but before they could grab him, he bolted through the open door. The man's ravings were cut short by a heavy thud. All of them ran onto the landing and looked down. Taschen lay sprawled on the floor, unmoving, neck twisted at an impossible angle. Zoe followed as the others ran down the stairs, her mind filled with the strange accusations Taschen had hurled at her. How did he know she wasn't who she seemed to be? And what did that have to do with the dark and the light? She hoped Elyana wouldn't take his words too seriously.

Niko bent to feel the old man's wrist for a pulse. It was no use. Blood pooled around his head.

"He's dead," Niko said.

"No!" Elyana screamed, shaking with sobs.

Zoe watched in surprise as the boy named Walker

put his arm around Elyana's shoulders and murmured gently to her.

"It was the dream water," Niko said sadly, closing Taschen's eyes. "There was nothing we could do. Someone gave him such a massive dose he would have died one way or the other. Even a few drops diluted in water is enough to make a person begin to forget who they are, to lose their will, and become what my master used to call a *nʒambi*, or walking no-soul."

No one said anything for a minute, as if mourning the life that had been lost. "Those things he said," Niko began slowly, looking at Zoe, "I wonder what he meant when he told you he knew who you really are. He looked as if his mind suddenly cleared at that moment."

Zoe's heart leaped into her throat. "He was crazy," she babbled. "Totally insane. He wasn't making any sense."

Niko stared at her, his gray eyes steely, and Zoe dropped her gaze. She didn't like the way he was sizing her up so suspiciously. But he didn't say anything else about it and neither did the others.

"We'd better get out of here before somebody comes," Niko said.

"Yeah. One thing I don't need is more trouble—or dead bodies attached to my name," Walker added under his breath.

Zoe looked at the boys curiously, but Elyana didn't seem to hear the boy's comment. There was something going on with these two . . . but they were right, the sooner they went their separate ways, the better. At least for tonight. She knew she'd be seeing this Walker again. After all, the Sisters had told her as much.

"Come on, Elyana. Let's go home," she said, without another look at the boys. Elyana was too dazed to do more than follow her cousin's lead. Zoe could only hope, as she and Elyana headed back to the Summerwynd estate, that none of them actually believed anything the old man said was true.

"Zecropia—I mean Zoe, I keep forgetting you prefer your nickname," Elyana began the next morning, as the two girls strolled along a white pebbled path that bordered the gardens of the estate. "Thank you for coming with me last night." She blinked back tears. "I just can't believe Taschen is gone."

Zoe nodded and looked toward the water where fishing boats were bobbing up and down on the smooth blue surface. The Summerwynd estate spanned one entire side of the harbor, a sprawling mansion of white granite and limestone, with bright pink and purple flowering vines adding splotches of color.

"It's so beautiful here," Zoe said to change the subject, trying to forget the crazed eyes of the old man and the things he had said.

Elyana nodded absently, twirling a strand of her long, flaming hair around one finger. "Listen, can you keep a secret?"

"Sure," Zoe said.

"So if I tell you something, you promise not to tell anyone? Especially not my father?"

Zoe nodded. Elyana certainly seemed to have a thing about keeping stuff from her father. Zoe'd only met him once when she arrived, a tall, perfectly groomed man who totally doted on his only daughter. Elyana leaned closer to Zoe and whispered in her ear. "I think I'm in love."

Zoe didn't say anything for a minute, just stared at her cousin in surprise. She didn't know what she'd been expecting the girl to say, but it wasn't this. "What do you mean?"

"Well, in my last reading, most of the bones fell inside the circle, which Taschen told me suggests intensity and conflict. Then I got a chain, which means a journey. And a cross, which has to do with crossroads or personal sacrifice. And then, this is the big thing, I got a letter, which I know stands for someone's name, and since my question was about love, I know it stands for the person I'm supposed to . . . well, the person who is the one for me. And the name of the person my father wants me to marry does not begin with *W.*"

"*W,*" Zoe echoed.

"I saw that boy before. I didn't know his name then— it was right before my last reading. I saw him out of my carriage window, our eyes met, and the way he looked at me made my stomach get all funny. And then last night after finding out his name, I understood my destiny."

"Last night?"

Elyana nodded, blushing. "You know, the boy named Walker."

Zoe breathed in sharply. This was terrible, worse than terrible. Elyana, who she was supposed to make sure married someone named Draco, was in love with someone else—in fact, the other person who had a role in her return home. It would be easier to get his charm if he and Elyana were together, but then what would that do to the whole Draco thing? No—if she ever wanted to go home, Zoe'd have to convince Elyana that Walker was not the one for her.

"Wait a minute," Zoe said quickly. "Don't you think maybe this is a case of pre-engagement jitters? I mean, you're probably nervous since you're supposed to meet your fiancé next week. So this boy comes along and you think you like him, but really you don't know anything about him. I mean, he could be an ax murderer, for all you know."

Elyana shook her head, blushing furiously. "He's not. He's special. But strangest of all, I feel as if I was supposed to meet him, as if it was my destiny. And I think he can feel it, too. Before you and I left them last night, he said he hoped to see me again."

Zoe sighed. This was worse than she had thought. "Listen, I don't know if I should tell you this because it's very sad, but another cousin of mine on my father's side . . ." Zoe's voice broke dramatically.

"What happened to her?" Elyana exclaimed, grasping Zoe's hands, her eyes wide.

"She had eloped with this traveling musician," Zoe elaborated, trying to come up with something romantic enough to catch Elyana's fancy. "See, the guy was really good-looking and a really smooth talker, and she fell for him in a big way. So he convinced her to steal some family heirlooms, which he reasoned would have been her dowry anyway, and then the two of them ran off to live happily ever after." Zoe paused, trying to come up with a truly horrible ending for her story.

"And then what happened?" Elyana breathed.

"It's really terrible. Are you sure you want to hear?" Elyana nodded.

"Well, he kept promising to marry her in the next town and the next. But he never did. And one day my cousin got fed up and they had this big fight and the musician hit her over the head with this huge silver teapot that had been her grandmother's, and he left her lying half dead in a ditch, and he took off with all of her family's heirlooms."

"Ooh," Elyana gasped. "How horrible! How is she now?"

"Well, she never got over it. The truth is, she went crazy. . . ." Zoe racked her brains for something even worse. ". . . And so they had to lock her up in the attic, and they can't let her out because whenever she hears music, it reminds her of the musician, and she goes into a frenzy and threatens to kill whoever is in the room with her."

"Oh, no!" Elyana gasped.

"Oh, yes," Zoe said. "So you see why I'm suspicious about this Walker. I just wouldn't want to see you running off into the sunset with the wrong person."

"But he's not like that. He's different. And I have to make Father understand."

Zoe sighed. This mission was turning out to be more and more impossible, but before she could even begin to reason with Elyana again, the gong rang signaling breakfast.

Zoe noticed in surprise that the table had been laid for three, which meant that Lyonel Summerwynd must be joining them. Moments after the girls took their seats, Lyonel Summerwynd appeared, looking more grave than usual. He didn't even sit down. Oh, no, Zoe thought, he knows. He knows I'm an impostor.

"I hate to ruin your breakfast, but there's been a murder," he said. "Two actually, and one on my ship, no less. So I don't want you girls to leave the grounds today. Is that understood?"

Zoe and Elyana glanced at each other, thinking of Taschen, then lowered their eyes.

"Who's been murdered, Father?" Elyana asked in a shaking voice.

"No one of importance," her father said dismissively. "And one of the dead, a bones reader, certainly was an evil person, dealing in black magic and trafficking with spirits. He doesn't concern me, except for the fact that the same person committed both crimes. But don't worry, we'll find him. I have an eyewitness who saw this boy at both crime scenes—and with a weapon in hand, no less."

"Boy?" Zoe echoed.

Lyonel Summerwynd nodded. "Yes, a stranger with yellow hair."

Elyana's eyes met Zoe's. Clearly they were both thinking the same thing.

"What will happen to him if . . . if you find him?"

"Well, he won't have long to live, if that's what you

mean. Death deserves death—that is how it has always been in Tyros."

Zoe smiled. So people thought the Bearer was a murderer. She didn't believe it—no way could she see that kid Walker killing anybody. Plus, she already knew he hadn't killed the bones guy. But it made getting the red charm suddenly seem possible, and Zoe thought she knew just how to do it.

CHAPTER 7

"I'm going to see Elyana and that's it," Walker announced, pacing the dusty floor of the cave. "You don't have to come with me if you don't want, but I'm going."

Niko sighed, exasperated, and shook his head. "It's not that. It's just— Well, Jek was murdered on her father's ship, and Ikbar did accuse you of the murder. . . ."

"So?" Walker burst out. "Elyana would never believe him! Especially after what happened last night with Taschen. I mean, he said the man with violet eyes was the one who gave him the dream water. She just has to help me."

Niko stared out of the cave entrance at the hot, starry darkness and sighed again. They'd been hiding out since leaving the bones reader's house late the night before. Far off an owl hooted, the eerie sound echoing in the stillness of the night.

"Are you sure you're not doing this for the wrong reasons?"

"What are you talking about?"

"Because you . . . er . . . because you have feelings for her . . ."

"Are you kidding?" Walker exploded, turning away so Niko wouldn't see him blush.

"No, I'm not. You told me you think she's beautiful—"

"Forget it," Walker cut in, blushing furiously. "I know what I said. And that doesn't have anything to do with it."

"Maybe not," Niko conceded thoughtfully. "But there's something else."

"What? Stop looking so mysterious and just spill it already."

"All right," Niko said slowly. "I don't think you should just blindly throw yourself on someone's mercy. I mean, you hardly know a thing about her, and even if she doesn't, her father probably thinks you're a . . ."

"Murderer," Walker finished, an angry flush climbing his cheeks. "That's right. Murderer. And it's me that's accused, not you, because I was the stupid one who grabbed the dagger and got blood all over myself. I think going to see Elyana is just about my only option. You can't possibly say anything bad about her. I mean, look how she tried to help that old bones reader when he was dying."

Niko nodded. "You may be right about *her*," he agreed. "But the other one, her cousin, has a strange energy field."

"Energy what? Speak English, please."

"Energy field. You know, aura."

"Give me a break, Niko. I don't believe in any of that weird New Age stuff."

"Well, I have a bad feeling about her."

"Oh, I see, and I'm supposed to make a decision which might affect the rest of my life—whether I even have a life—based on a feeling of yours about someone's energy field. I don't think so."

"It was more than a feeling. It was an instinct, and my master always told me to trust my instincts."

"Well, I don't believe in instincts. I believe in proof. Cold, hard, empirical proof. And you have no proof that Zoe is out to get me. Do you?"

Niko shook his head. "You don't understand."

"But I do," Walker sputtered. "I understand that the concept of justice, of being innocent until proven guilty, is completely alien in a place like this. I bet they hang or draw and quarter murderers with no trial, no lawyers, no nothing. And I'm not taking that chance, okay? So I'm going to see Elyana and see if she'll help me. If you want to stay here in this hot, stupid, smelly cave, then that's fine with me."

Without a backward glance Walker strode out of the cave and headed down the dusty path leading toward Tyros and Elyana Summerwynd. In less than five paces he felt Niko fall into step beside him.

"Maybe you're right," Niko said, without looking at his friend.

"I guess we'll find out," Walker answered.

And that was all they said as they made their way toward the lights below.

The city of Tyros was filled with activity for so late in the evening. A frantic bustling buzzed through the entire place like an electrical current. Soldiers were searching from house to house, while horsemen patrolled the streets.

"Whoa!" Walker exclaimed as he and Niko ducked into an alley to avoid the thundering hoofbeats and searching eyes of one of the patrolling parties.

When they emerged a few minutes later, Walker saw something that made his heart stop. He pointed slowly, and Niko, who was busy casing the street for searchers, turned to look. There on the side of the building before them was a poster with a crude drawing of Walker and a caption: Wanted for Murder. His nose might have been too big, but other than that it was dead-on. He shuddered at his unfortunate choice of words.

Just then another search party made its way down the street. The two boys flattened themselves against the wall. Luckily for them this search party was not very thorough and charged off in the opposite direction after the briefest look.

"That was close," Walker said, finally letting out his breath.

Niko nodded grimly as they continued on their way, making sure to avoid the main streets. After that, neither of them said a word. When they finally reached the harbor, they ducked behind a storage shed near the long stone bridge that spanned the bay. The Summerwynd estate was on the other side. There were soldiers everywhere. In the orange glare of the torches that dotted the bridge, soldiers appeared to be stopping every person who tried to cross in either direction.

"Now what are we going to do?" Walker asked. "I mean what am *I* going to do?" It wasn't Niko's problem after all.

"Try and get through the checkpoint," Niko suggested.

"How are we going to do that? They know exactly what I look like. You saw the poster."

Niko nodded. "That's why you need a disguise."

"What kind of disguise?"

Niko frowned, his brows drawn together in thought. "You could be a girl," he finally said.

"No way!" Walker burst out. "I'm not going to do that."

"All right. Then we swim across."

Both boys looked at the water, watching as the ocean tide met the flow of the river, where it created a swirling, rushing effect like a whirlpool, the water dark and frothing. Dangerous even for the most skilled swimmers.

Walker turned to Niko, a resigned expression on his face. "All right. You win. I'll be a girl. But you'd better not laugh at me. You swear?"

Niko nodded, suppressing a smile. "I swear. Now wait here while I go get what we need to . . . er . . . to bring out your feminine side."

Walker shook his head and crouched in the shadows. At first, waiting wasn't so bad, but as more time passed, the reality of his situation, of the danger he was in, began to overtake him, and he started thinking of home. Of his mom and his dog, Blue. Even of his older brother, Bo, who always picked on him. He hadn't thought about home in a long time. He'd been too busy. First, escaping from the Dragon training camp at Black Rock, then going through the ring of lights to this world, then losing the charm, and Jek's murder. Now, for the first time, he felt afraid. Afraid he might never see his home again. He didn't hear Niko coming down the alleyway toward him. Hurriedly, he wiped his eyes with his sleeve.

"Walker," Niko said gently. "Here."

He held out a sleeveless blue dress and a pair of slippers with flowers on the toes. Then he held up a jar of black goo.

"That smells nasty," Walker remarked, wrinkling his nose. "What do you plan to do with it?"

"You'll see," Niko said, grinning.

"How'd you get all this stuff anyway?"

Niko didn't answer, just busied himself stirring the black goo with one finger. "Put on the dress, okay?" Walker was studying Niko, wondering, when he noticed that Niko's good green cloak was gone. So that was how he'd afforded the dress. Niko had traded the only valuable thing he had.

"Thanks, bro," he murmured over his shoulder, too softly for Niko to hear. Then he slipped off his tunic and pants and pulled the dress over his head. It bunched up under his armpits, but he was able to yank it down so that it fell to his knees. It was tight around the waist and loose at the top but it was close enough. He turned to Niko, who bit his lip and looked away.

"What?"

"I don't know. I guess you just . . . you make a

very . . . uh . . . strange-looking girl. But don't worry. Maybe this will help." He dipped his fingers into the black goo and then rubbed his hands together, reaching for Walker's head.

"Hey, what do you think you're doing?"

"I'm going to change the color of your hair."

"Gross." But Walker submitted, allowing Niko to work the stinky black stuff through his hair.

"Perfect," Niko said, stepping back to survey his handiwork.

"Except for one thing," Walker said, pulling out the slack material at the top of the dress where a woman's chest would have filled it out. "It'll never work."

"Yes, it will. I'll show you." Niko picked up Walker's discarded tunic and carefully tore off a section of the material. Then he rolled it into a ball and stuffed it inside the dress. He put another wad of material on the other side. "There."

Walker stared down at his now bulging chest and grinned. "I look pretty good, huh?"

Niko smiled as he tore off another section of material. This one he carefully folded into a triangle. "Wrap this around your head."

"Why?" Walker asked, frowning as he took the material.

"Just do it," Niko said.

Awkwardly, Walker fumbled with the cloth, finally

managing to get it over his hair and tying it behind his head.

"What's it supposed to do, anyway?"

"Hide the fact that your hair isn't very long. Now put on the slippers."

Walker grimaced, trying to work his large feet into the dainty flowered shoes. He was just about able to do it, but they pinched awfully over the toes. Niko looked him up and down.

"I think it might work," Niko said with a grin. "Just don't talk."

"Very funny," Walker said.

"Okay. Let's go."

The boys slipped out from the safety of the shed and headed toward the main street that led to the bridge. As they drew closer, the crowd swelled. Soldiers were stationed at both ends, silver helmets on their heads, swords at their belts, and eyes trained warily on the crowd, searching for the murderer.

"Everyone must be checked before they can cross!" shouted one of the guards.

The crowd buzzed with impatience.

"Can you believe all this, missy?" exclaimed a man with a ring of tools around his waist. "This could take all night." The man shook his head at Walker, looked him quickly up and down, and then winked.

"Hey!" Walker began in his normal voice, before

catching himself and turning the word into a fit of coughing.

"You all right, missy?" the man asked, leaning closer.

The guy was flirting! Walker thought in horror, and although he felt like punching him, he just nodded his head in agreement and began to back away.

"What are they looking for anyway?" the man inquired, his beady eyes still on Walker.

"A murderer," Niko said, coming to Walker's rescue. "Let's go this way, Mina." Niko grabbed Walker by the hand and pulled him away from the man.

"Disgusting!" Walker exploded. "That guy was—"

"What? Treating you like a girl?" There was mischief in Niko's eyes.

Walker nodded. "Well, I guess we know one thing—the disguise works."

"Or that man was totally desperate. Either way, it was a close one."

After that, Walker and Niko stood quietly in line, slowly inching their way to the checkpoint. They watched as soldiers looked at each pedestrian, then at a piece of paper, obviously the poster with Walker's picture on it.

As they moved closer to the checkpoint, Walker wanted to change plans. "Let's separate," he whispered. "It'll be safer."

"No," Niko said.

"Yes," Walker insisted. "If my disguise doesn't work, at least you'll be free."

Niko was about to open his mouth to object, but Walker was too fast for him. He pushed into the surging crowd, elbowing his way to the front of the line. He bumped into someone and nearly lost his balance.

"Excuse me," Walker squealed in a high-pitched voice.

"Sure, miss," said the man, reaching out an arm to steady Walker.

Walker cringed but didn't push the man away. He just smiled quickly and moved a few steps back. He could barely believe it, but maybe the disguise really was going to work.

Three people ahead. Then two. Then one.

"Next!" barked the guard in a rough voice.

Walker took a deep breath and sauntered up to the guard, trying to walk lightly on his toes like a girl, while at the same time keeping the slippers on, a difficult task since his feet kept slipping out of them.

"Where are you from, girl?" the guard asked brusquely, squinting as he peered at Walker, his hand on the sword at his hip.

"From the North," Walker replied in a falsetto voice, batting his eyelashes at the same time.

"What brings you here to Tyros?" the guard continued, frowning and wrinkling his nose after getting a whiff of the black goo in Walker's hair.

"What brings me to Tyros . . . ?" Walker repeated, trying to think of something to say that would sound reasonably true. "What brings every girl to Tyros?" He batted his eyelashes at the guard once more.

The guard stared at him, a puzzled expression on his face.

"Finding a man," Walker finally blurted out, deciding the guard must be pretty thick. "That's what brings me to Tyros."

Some of the other guards began to laugh. "Well, you gonna have a heck of a time doin' that," said one. And the other guards laughed along with him.

"Fresh!" Walker exclaimed.

"Let her pass," the first guard said, still not quite getting the joke. The others hooted and catcalled, but Walker didn't care. He was going to make it! He couldn't believe it.

"Thank you," he tossed over his shoulder, giving a little wave that he thought was suitably flirtatious. Then he began to make his way from the checkpoint toward the bridge, which loomed just ahead. He was almost there. Just a few more steps and he'd be on his way to Elyana. In his excitement Walker didn't notice that one of the balls of material wadded up in his dress had fallen to the ground by the checkpoint.

"Miss, you dropped something!" the guard shouted after him.

He froze, debating whether to make a run for it or to turn around, and decided in that one agonizing second that it would seem too suspicious if he just took off. Slowly he turned back toward the guard, who held out the material. He stared at Walker's chest, his mouth hanging open in surprise. Walker looked down to see what the matter was, and all the color drained from his face. He had only one breast! The other was wadded up in the guard's hand. Illumination spread across the guard's heavy, plain features.

"Seize him!" he shouted, pointing at Walker.

Soldiers from the bridge ahead and the street behind all moved toward him, swords and daggers drawn. Cornered like a mouse by a pack of hungry cats, Walker did the only thing he could think of—he jumped off the bridge into the swirling water below.

CHAPTER 8

Niko sighed as he crested the hill. It was silent but for the soughing of wind through the dark, twisting street. Still, he couldn't shake the feeling that he was being followed, that one of the guards from the bridge had noticed him with Walker and given chase. He glanced back once but saw nothing except the broken-down wooden houses that bordered the alley on both sides. He was almost there.

An owl cried and Niko jumped, the hair on the back of his neck prickling. Hurrying around the corner, he saw the house just ahead, the dark triangular symbol on the door clear in the moonlight. It was the only place he could think of where no one would bother him and where he could rest for a few hours and maybe, just maybe, Walker would think to go.

An image of the dark swirling water popped into his mind, but he willed it away. Walker couldn't be dead.

From somewhere behind him came a rustling. Without looking to see who or what it was, Niko pushed open the door of the bones reader's house and slipped inside, closing it softly behind him. He stood there, heart beating fast in his chest, listening, but there was no sound from outside. The guard, or whoever he thought had been following him, seemed to be gone.

He decided to go upstairs to Taschen's study. When he got to the top of the steps, he pushed open the study door. A faint sweet and spicy scent still lingered in the air—the dream water. The room was just as he had seen it last, with overturned bookcases, ruined parchments, and broken chairs. As he surveyed the damage, the closet door suddenly opened, and a dark shape stepped forward into the moonlight. Niko gasped.

"So we meet again, boy," rasped the harsh, horrible voice of the cloaked man from the ship, the trader known as Ikbar. His hood fell away as he leaned toward Niko, revealing his strange violet eyes.

Niko backed away and tripped on a pile of books. At the same time, the clatter of horseshoes on stone sounded just outside the window. Ikbar moved toward the door and jammed a chair under the latch. "One word from me, murderer . . ." He paused on the word, and a terrible smile lit up his ghostly face. ". . . and they will be on you like vultures on a dead thing. Oh, I know you're not the one accused of the crime, but I could make it quite clear that you were a willing accomplice. Unless, of course, you agree to do as I say. The choice is yours . . . Chooser."

"What do you mean?" Niko tried not to sound afraid, but the words came out in a shaky croak.

"I am a magic seeker, one of the last of the Skyggni. I want the magic that comes of you being the Chooser. Your magic is more subtle than a charm but no less powerful, and I know of those who would be most interested to discover it for themselves. Therefore, my proposition is this. Allow—"

Ikbar's words were cut off by the sounds of men dismounting.

"They will be on to you in a matter of moments. Agree to do what I want, and I will restore you to your friend. If not, I will turn you in."

Niko's mind whirled and his heart pounded. He didn't trust Ikbar for one minute, but he didn't know what other choice he had. "What do you want me to do?"

"Answer a few questions. Then I will take you to your friend."

"How do I know you even know where he is?" Niko countered. "And why should I trust you?"

Ikbar shrugged and said nothing as downstairs the

front door was thrown open with a bang. Footsteps thundered up the stairs and then swords hammered against the study door.

"No harm will come to you, I can assure you of that." Ikbar's violet eyes were not reassuring in the slightest.

Feeling as if he had no choice, Niko was just about to nod his agreement when the door splintered apart and a swarm of guards barreled inside, swords flashing. At the same time a green light filled the room, and the soldiers froze in place, weapons raised, eyes open but unblinking, staring at nothing. All movement and noise ceased—except for Niko's rapid breathing.

The light seemed to swirl into itself and contract until a woman with flowing golden hair and eyes as blue as sapphires emerged. Niko stared in openmouthed wonder. He had seen the glowing green light once before in his master's study.

"Come with me, Niko," the woman said in a soft voice that brought goose bumps to Niko's arms. "Do not be afraid. I am Calliope, Sister of the Kuxan-Sunn, and I am here to help you assist the Protector in recovering the charms."

Niko blinked, as much surprised by the kind tone of the spirit woman as he was by her words.

"Don't listen to her," Ikbar sputtered with a harsh

laugh. "She is a Sister and well trained in the arts of dissimulation—heartless and devious, intent only on interfering with the destiny of man for her own selfish ends."

"It is true that some of my Sisters have less than honorable intentions," Calliope answered in her smooth, silky voice. "But I am not like them, which is why I have come—to show you the way to Aurora and the charms."

"She lies, boy. Don't let her cunning manipulate you. It is one of the tricks of the spirits to lure men off their path."

Niko stared from Calliope to Ikbar and back. He didn't know whom to believe. He had no reason to trust Ikbar, certainly, who had already killed two innocent men in cold blood. But Calliope's green glow and his memory of that night at the castle and the sad look on his master's face kept rising up in his brain like some kind of warning.

"Come, Niko. The black dragon's power grows stronger with each passing day. Soon it may have what it needs to rise again. You must help to stop it, Chooser of the nine charms of the Lords of Time."

He frowned, paralyzed with indecision.

"I cannot keep the guards at bay much longer." Calliope's smooth-as-silk voice rustled through the room.

"Don't listen to her," Ikbar warned, his violet eyes intent on Niko's. "Didn't your master ever tell you not to trust anyone whose hand you can't shake?"

Niko's mind whirled in an agony of indecision. He was almost ready to go with Ikbar, if the trader could really take him to Walker, when Ikbar grabbed his arm. "She lies, foolish boy, and you are too stupid to see. But I have no more time to wait. The choice is mine, Chooser. You come with me."

In that instant, Niko knew that going with Ikbar was exactly the wrong choice. "No!" he yelled, digging his feet into the floor as the cloaked man tried to drag him away.

Suddenly there was an explosion of green light. Niko felt hot and cold simultaneously, drowning in green air, and thought he was about to die. There was a roar in his ears, and then he blacked out. When he came to, he was lying on the floor of the cave in the mountains where he had first hidden with Walker. He sat up slowly, blinking to adjust to the gloom, his head throbbing and his limbs as rubbery as if he'd run a great distance. Before him stood Calliope, a look of concern on her pale, beautiful face.

"I had to dematerialize you. I'm sorry, but the trader Ikbar left me no choice—he is a renegade Skyggni with enough dark magic to cause great harm. I was powerless to do anything, of course, until you decided to trust me. A simple emotion—trust—and one which I have come to understand and value above almost all others. My Sisters do not feel any emotions, you know. I trained myself to do so only after much study of your race and even then . . . but that is not the point."

"What happened?" Niko asked, standing slowly and rubbing his temples.

"There is no time for explanations. Aurora needs you. You are safe from Ikbar and the guards for the time being. And now you must go back to your world."

"But what about Walker?" Niko blurted out.

Calliope shook her head and her hair rippled like golden sunlight shimmering on water. "It is not your destiny. The Bearer must walk his way alone."

"But he's my friend. That's not fair, or right."

"The worlds of man, Chooser, are neither fair nor right, which is why it is up to you to bring the light once more into balance with the dark. You know the prophecy?"

Niko shook his head.

"Did your master not tell you the story of the Lords of Time?"

"Only that people used to believe there were such beings, and that they forged the nine charms as keepers of the light. That's about all I know, except for the fact that the charms have a Chooser, a Protector, and a Bearer."

"There is more, much more, but we only have time

for the barest details." With that, Calliope fixed her sapphire eyes on Niko and began to speak in her soft, musical voice, but this time with an urgency Niko hadn't heard before:

> *"Nine were the charms,*
> *golden-silver, made of light,*
> *forged by the Lords of Time*
> *to help take back the night."*

"Wait!" Niko interrupted. "I know that. It's a nursery rhyme."

"No, it's not," Calliope said. "It is the prophecy. And it is as real as you are."

With that, she continued and Niko listened, remembering the night he and Aurora had first found the charms hidden in the hilt of Janus's silver sword, and how the two of them had recited the rhyme—as best as they could recall it—together.

> *"Each of these nine lords*
> *one color charm did hold,*
> *to fight the darkness rising,*
> *or so the story's told.*

> *But long ago the nine were lost,*
> *the Lords of Time all passed.*

Dark and light made an uneasy truce,
but never would that last.
One must find the nine,
one must have the power,
and one will come from somewhere else
to fight the Dark Lord's hour.

Silver will be his sword,
silver like his eyes.
The choosing of the charms
is where his skill lies."

Calliope paused then and smiled at Niko. "You see why I say the prophecy is real, for are you not the Chooser, and do you not possess a silver sword?"

"I did, but I lost it. I mean, it was stolen."

Calliope shook her head so that her golden hair shimmered. "What is lost can be found. Now listen carefully, for I do not know if you have ever heard the rest of the prophecy in its true form."

"Sign of the Dragon's Eye,
great will be her sight.
She is the Protector,
the guardian of the light."

Calliope paused again. "Aurora," Niko murmured.

*"From another world
where magic is no more,
his task shall be to fight
for the light in the coming war.
Called by all the Bearer,
The white dragon holds the key
to find the Chooser and Protector
and form the Circle of Three."*

"What white dragon?" Niko interrupted. "I mean, I know the Bearer is Walker, but I don't see how the white dragon has anything to do with him finding Aurora and me. I told you I should go to him. Then the two of us can—"

"Listen to the rest," Calliope cut in.

*"But if a second Bearer
by the dark is then called forth,
the black dragon shall be freed
from its prison in the North.
And the Bearer of the Dark
shall face the Bearer of the Light.
The white dragon must be risen
or all shall be endless night."*

Niko frowned, thinking hard. "So you're saying that the dark sent out a charm and called forth a second

Bearer, who is going to face off against Walker. Okay, I understand that, I think. But what about the dragons? There are no such things any longer."

"During the reign of the Lords of Time, two mortal kings shared power over all the worlds, each possessing a dragon as his mascot. The black dragon king decided that he wanted all the power for himself, so he killed the white dragon king and stole the charms. He didn't act alone, however; a dark sorcerer talked him into doing it, pushing him to the ways of the darkness. Eventually the charms were taken back by the evil sorcerer's opposite—Lord Amber, the sorcerer of light."

"Lord Amber, my master?" Niko exclaimed in surprise.

Calliope nodded.

"When you chose the sword, Niko, you set the ancient prophecy into motion. The light must once again do battle with the dark and finally put the black dragon and its new king to rest, along with the evil sorcerer who turned him to darkness. Aurora is at their mercy, as are the charms, and only you can stop them."

"Where are they?"

"At a place in the North, on the far reaches of the Cold Edge. Are you familiar with the Crystal Claw Mountains in the Dark Peaks?"

Niko nodded, remembering his geography lessons with Lord Amber.

"There is a fortress there called Nine Shadows Henge, an ancient stone place older than the mountains themselves. There, in the Great Age, it is said, the nine charms were kept. It is a sacred place, a magic place, and you must be very careful, for its magic has been turned to the dark."

"How am I to get back there?"

"The same way you got here. Come. We must hurry."

Niko took one last look around the cave and followed Calliope through the gray light of early morning, along the dusty mountain path flanked by red sandstone mountains. Calliope murmured some words in a language Niko had never heard before and moved her hands in a complicated series of gestures. Then before his eyes appeared the same glittering ring of lights he had traveled through with Walker. He could see the yellow sands of the desert and feel the hot, dry wind of his world on the other side.

"Go, Chooser, before it is too late."

As he stared through the glimmering lights, a small dappled pony trotted into view, saddled with bags on either side.

"Your mount awaits. He is of northern stock and knows the way you must go."

Niko nodded, took a deep breath, and stepped through the lights into the hot, dry desert. He squinted in the bright light as the intense heat enveloped him. The pony trotted up to him and stood waiting for him to mount. Niko turned as the sparkling lights began to fade from view, and as he watched, the door in the air disappeared and the world of Tyros along with it. Taking a deep breath, he mounted the pony and began to ride away, trying not to think about Walker and the world he had left behind.

Suddenly the pony reared high in the air. Niko grabbed the reins just in time to prevent himself from falling.

"Hey, new boy! Where do you think you're going?"

Niko whirled around. Behind him on horseback were two of the novices he'd met at Black Rock. The squat one he remembered was named Bram, and the lanky, pale-eyed one was Olan. Niko kicked his legs into the pony's sides. "Come on!" he urged, leaning into her neck.

The pony began to gallop, and the novices charged after them. The pony was fast, and Niko might have gotten away if the boys hadn't been throwing rocks. One rock caught his mount on the shin, and she reared again, whinnying. Niko once more had to use all his strength to keep from tumbling to the ground.

"It's all right, girl," he said soothingly. Then he saw the bleeding gash on her leg. As the rocks rained down around them, she tried to gallop on, but another rock caught her in the ear, and she bucked so hard that Niko was thrown. He spit out a mouthful of sand, then he saw that Bram and Olan had reined in on either side of him.

"So, new boy, where's your friend?"

Niko shrugged but didn't answer. He knew he was at a disadvantage because he was down and also because he was tired from lack of sleep. His reflexes were off, and without them, he was as sad as their prisoner.

Olan dismounted and kicked Niko hard in the stomach. Niko doubled over in pain but didn't allow Olan the satisfaction of letting out even a tiny groan.

"We know you went through some kinda door in the desert with that recruit, Walker. And we know you just came back through the same door. We saw the lights, but they was gone so fast—like magic, right, Bram?"

Bram laughed and edged his horse closer. Beyond him Niko spotted his pony, which was licking her leg but appeared otherwise unhurt.

"We promised Marcus we'd find the door you went through, and you're gonna help us. So open up that door again so we can go through it."

"I can't."

"Whaddya mean, ya can't? You went through it twice, so you must know how to make it appear."

Niko shook his head and Olan kicked him again.

"If you won't open the door, then you leave me and my friend no choice," Olan hissed in a harsh, horrible voice.

"Wh-what do you mean?"

"I mean that we'll just have to take you back to the House of the Black Rock, that's what."

Niko shook his head. "No, you can't. I have to go." He made as if to stand up and Olan pushed him down.

"Not so fast, new boy. Like I said, you either open that door or . . ." Olan let his words trail off while Bram dismounted and came to stand on Niko's other side. Bram kicked Niko in the head while Olan kicked him in the legs and stomach—until Niko heard himself groan in pain. He thought as he lay there in the burning sun, his head spinning and his body on fire, that Calliope was wrong and he wasn't the one who could stop the black dragon, because he was about to die.

"Hey, what's that?" Bram cried in alarm.

All three boys stopped and looked. Niko blinked blearily as something dark hurtled out of the sky. Niko closed his eyes, sure the thing was going to land on him and kill him, when he heard a familiar *cak-cak* cry. The bird dove down, landing on Olan's head, talons ripping at his hair. Before the startled boy could do more than gasp, the bird had soared back up into the air. Then she plummeted to attack Bram. Both boys fell away, their screams echoing along with the *cak-cak* of the bird.

Niko stared at the bird, wondering, but as soon as it trained its golden yellow eyes on him, he knew—it was Topaz, and she had found him, just as Aurora had predicted. At that moment he knew with certainty that he would indeed make it to Nine Shadows Henge to fulfill his destiny as the Chooser of the nine charms.

CHAPTER 9

Walker clutched the driftwood tightly as another wave washed over him. Shivering, he spit the saltwater out of his mouth and gasped for air. In the distance rose the black silhouette of the bridge, and all around it, fanning out on both sides of the harbor, orange points of light bobbed in the darkness. Boats. The faint shouting of the guards calling to each other drifted toward him. They'd soon be searching for his corpse—he didn't know how much longer he could hold on like this. He was so cold and tired. Longingly he stared at the seawall lined with mansions. One of those houses was Elyana's, but the nearest house was at least half a mile away, which was seventy-something laps in an Olympic-sized pool, he remembered from his days on the swim team.

He must have fallen asleep, because the next thing he knew, there was a shout as a voice called out, "Over there! By the driftwood!"

Walker looked up. The voice had come from a small boat heading his way. He'd have to do something if he didn't want to be seen. He dove beneath the water and swam under the driftwood to the opposite side, and not a moment too soon. Shielded by gnarled roots that rose up almost like a sail, he watched as the orange glow of a torch flickered over the very spot where he had just been floating. Suddenly the boat bumped into the driftwood and Walker lost his hold. He sank under the water, and when he came up, reaching out to grab his makeshift life preserver, he heard someone say, "Ridiculous. Let's go back."

"No," said another voice, this one high and sweet yet firm. "He's out here somewhere."

Walker started in surprise. Those voices sounded familiar. But what would Elyana and Zoe be doing out on the water at this time of night? He must be hearing wrong. But when he craned his neck to see, there was Elyana, her pale face frowning in the light of the torch Zoe was holding. Walker opened his mouth to shout out when a wave rolled over him and he swallowed another mouthful of water. Coughing and sputtering, he forced himself back to the surface.

"Elyana!" He tried to yell, but his voice was faint and his lungs were still filled with water and instead he began to cough.

"Who's that?" Elyana called out. "Walker, is that you?"

"It was just the wave," Zoe said.

"Ely—" Walker tried again, but he was overcome with a fit of coughing.

And then something even worse happened. A large boat with a figurehead in the shape of a roaring lion came into view, heading right for them, rowed by lines of men with long oars slap-slapping the water. It reminded Walker of a Viking galley, sleek, fast, and carrying a whole bunch of men as vicious looking as the lion they rowed behind.

"Prepare to be boarded!" called a deep voice.

Within seconds, the galley was alongside. Soldiers jumped off the deck onto the smaller craft.

"What is the meaning of this?" Elyana cried.

Walker held his breath, staying as still as possible.

"Lady Elyana, you are in grave danger," announced a commanding voice from the ship. Walker figured it must be the captain. "There's a murderer on the loose and your father thought . . ."

The rest of the captain's words were drowned out by the arrival of another big wave, which made the smaller boat list sharply to one side. Walker went under for a second, and when he came up, Elyana was leaning over the side, trying to regain her balance. Their eyes met at the same moment that someone on board called out, "Sir, I see something. Floating on the other side of the driftwood."

Walker gulped, his stomach flip-flopping. He was in for it now. There was nowhere left to hide, unless he stayed under, but he didn't know how long he could hold his breath.

"Captain!" Elyana said in an imperious tone. "You can take us to shore, as the night cruise I was conducting for my cousin has been ruined."

"Your Ladyship, I do not think—"

"Precisely. You did not think, and as a result my cousin and I have had our cruise ruined, a fact which my father will be very unhappy to learn. Now tow us back to land." She stared defiantly up at the captain, her hands on her hips, one loose lock of red hair blowing in the wind.

The captain bowed and signaled for his men to return to their boat. Way to go, Elyana! Walker cheered silently, watching as a rope was tied to the bow of the pleasure boat. Then the galley turned and began to pull the girls away. Now what? Walker wondered. He watched the boats moving farther away, his spirits plummeting. Maybe Elyana hadn't really seen him and he'd just thought she had. As if in answer, Elyana quickly lowered something over the side of her boat.

A rope, Walker realized, and swam hard to reach it. He held on as best he could, but his fingers were cold and stiff and they kept slipping. Hang on, he told himself as his fingers began to burn from the chafing of the rope. He did his best not to think about anything other than finally getting to dry land. Walker had no idea how much time passed, but eventually he could see what he assumed was the Summerwynd mansion just ahead. He watched as Elyana moved to the bow, untied the rope that bound her boat to the bigger ship, and with a nod to the captain threw it into the water.

The captain bowed and stood watching the smaller craft make its way through the narrow channel to the Summerwynds' dock. But he gave no signal for the galley to leave. What is he waiting for? Walker wondered in panic.

"Thank you, Captain!" Elyana called out. "We can manage from here."

The captain nodded, but he still stood staring after the girls' boat. Uh-oh, thought Walker. Maybe he saw me. Better not risk it. He took a deep breath at the same moment the captain signaled to hook the rope Walker was holding. Just in time, Walker let go and dove into

the water. When he came up for air, he saw in relief that
the larger boat was pulling away.

"Ouch!" Walker sputtered as Zoe grabbed on to his
clothes and pulled him roughly out of the water.

"You're alive!" Elyana exclaimed, helping to lay him
gently on the ground. "Do you feel all right?"

Walker nodded, trying to stop his teeth from chat-
tering. "You . . . saved . . . my life and—"

"What are you doing in a dress?" Zoe interrupted.
"I mean, is that what you—"

The rest of her sentence was cut off by the thundering of hoofbeats.

"More soldiers!" Elyana said, starting in alarm. "It
means they're still looking for—"

"Me," Walker supplied wearily. "You know I didn't
do it, right?"

Elyana nodded, her green eyes wide with sympathy.

"It was Ikbar, the trader. He killed Jek on your father's ship. And he killed Taschen, too."

"I know," Elyana said. "I realized that last night. But
you must hide now." Gently she pulled Walker to his
feet. "Until I can talk to my father and explain that this
Ikbar is the real criminal. We must hurry. Follow me."

"Yeah," agreed Zoe. "If these soldiers get you,
you're dead."

Elyana led them to a boathouse, a mini trellised version of the main house, with columns and urns and even a small fountain in front. And not a moment too soon. Walker turned back to see soldiers like menacing black shadows in the creepy orange torchlight, spilling onto the Summerwynds' patio.

"There's a secret room through here," Elyana whispered, motioning them inside. "It was my mother's. She used to take me when I was small. No one knows about it—not even my father."

Moonlight spilled from the floor-to-ceiling windows that ran the length of the main room of the boathouse, casting silver puddles of light. Huddled under canvas were bulky shapes, their tall masts sticking out at the top. Next, they passed into a room filled with oars and tackle boxes, then another with coils of rope and boxes of wax and washing supplies. Finally, they came to a solid stone wall that marked the end of the boathouse. Elyana stopped, studying the wall, and Walker wondered if she was getting cold feet. Zoe must have wondered too, because she looked over at him and shrugged her shoulders.

"Elyana," Zoe began, just as Elyana stretched out one hand. She moved it to the right, paused to chew on a fingernail, then moved it a bit farther, until it rested on a flat gray stone no bigger or smaller than the rest of the stones that made up the wall. She pushed on another stone about five stones above the first and another five stones to the left. And then before Walker's astonished eyes, a secret door swung open.

"Whoa!" Walker exclaimed as Zoe gasped in surprise.

Elyana shot them a quick smile and then beckoned them forward, stopping to light a candle she pulled from her pocket. She led them down a steep flight of narrow stairs that were thick with dust and cobwebs. Eventually the ground leveled off, and they found themselves in a wide passageway with a low, sloping roof that reminded Walker of the tunnels through the canyons in Malibu.

"What is this place?" he asked after they'd been walking for some time.

"It was used during the Great War to move troops and supplies," Elyana explained. "The other entrance is deep in the forest. Where we're going shouldn't be much farther."

Before long the path split into three. Elyana chose the leftmost tunnel and followed it to the end, where it opened into a hall with a high ceiling. Inside were stacks of wooden crates marked with the sigil of the white lily.

"Those are Father's crates!" Elyana blurted out in surprise.

"They look like the ones we were unloading the

other day," Walker said. "But I thought they were all being put in the warehouse at the dock."

"That's where they always go," Elyana said slowly. "I don't understand how they could have gotten here. No one uses this passageway."

"Apparently someone does," Zoe put in.

"But who?"

The image of Ikbar's strange violet eyes flashed into Walker's mind as he remembered the terrible scene in the hold, the pools of blood everywhere, the little green bottle. "Dream water," Walker burst out. "I found dream water in the crates on your father's ship. Suppose these are those crates. What better place to hide them than in the praefectus's house?"

Elyana's eyes widened in horror.

"Well, there's only one way to find out," Zoe said matter-of-factly. "Let's open one."

When much pulling and grunting had no effect on one crate, Walker got the idea to bang a rock on its corner. After a number of blows the top loosened, and the three of them were able to slide it off. A fishy smell wafted off the skins inside.

"It's just a bunch of skins," Zoe said, wrinkling her nose.

"Maybe not," Walker countered. He began tossing the stinking pelts to the floor, with Elyana working hard beside him. When they had emptied almost the entire crate, they found exactly what he thought they might— a small, delicately chiseled, blue glass bottle with a tiny stopper, this one in the shape of a flower. The three of them were so intent on their discovery that they didn't notice the shadow slipping silently into the hall behind them.

Zoe reached for the bottle.

"Don't touch it!" Walker barked, grabbing her arm. "It's dangerous."

But Zoe didn't listen. She clutched the bottle and held it up to the light.

"Dream water," Elyana murmured. "But what is it doing here? My father would never traffic in magic. It's illegal."

"Wait a minute," Walker said slowly, thinking aloud. "I bet that Ikbar hid these crates here. He's probably starting a smuggling ring and using your father's cargo as cover for his illegal activities, like importing dream water."

"That's terrible," Elyana burst out. "I must tell Father."

Walker didn't say anything, but he couldn't help but wonder if Elyana's father would believe her. After all, he seemed pretty happy with Ikbar and his great cargo—which reminded Walker of something else.

Glancing quickly at Elyana and then away, Walker said, "So I hear you're going to get married."

Elyana blushed. "Well, I haven't said 'yes' yet, if that's what you mean."

Walker couldn't stop the smile that sprang to his lips.

"I mean, I haven't even met him yet," she went on. "He's supposed to arrive in Tyros any day now. Then I'll see."

"I still don't get how a little bottle of perfume like this could have killed that old guy," Zoe cut in, studying the bottle.

"I don't understand how it could, either," Walker added, "but Niko said it makes you see stuff, like visions. And I guess it makes you lose your mind somehow."

Elyana nodded. "That's why it's so dangerous. Less than a drop can make you lose all touch with reality. A whole bottle . . ." Elyana shuddered and looked away.

"Really," Zoe said, her eyes fastened on the bottle with a burning interest.

"Put it back," Walker ordered.

To his surprise, Zoe actually listened to him. She bent over the crate and carefully placed the blue bottle back where they'd found it. "Hand me the pelts," she called over her shoulder.

Walker and Elyana bent at the same moment to pick

up the skins. Neither saw Zoe snatch the little blue bottle and stash it in her pocket. Walker did, however, notice the gloating smile on her face.

"What's so funny?" he asked.

Zoe just shrugged. "Nothing," she said as she absently stuck her hand in the pocket of her dress.

They left the hall and headed back the way they had come. They eventually came to where the path split into three tunnels. Again they came to a dead end and Elyana slid her hands over the stones, pushing one here, another there, in some special order. A door opened, revealing a curving set of dusty stone steps. The three began to climb, first Elyana, then Walker, then Zoe, around and around as the stairs wound upward. At the top was a door made of white wood.

Slowly Elyana pushed the door open. By the flickering light of the candle Walker could see they were in a round room made of white stone. Everything was white—the furniture, the walls, the floor, as well as things covered in white sheets he assumed must be more furniture. Elyana walked into the center of the room and stared down at the floor, a strange, faraway look in her eyes. Walker followed her gaze and saw that set into the stone was a mosaic of a magnificent white dragon sheathed in gold, its eyes blazing blue, its mouth open wide, shooting crimson and orange flames. But it was the stones around the dragon that caught Walker's attention.

"What is this place?" Zoe asked.

Elyana pointed to the floor. "My mother always called it the tower of the white dragon."

After the girls left, Walker slipped into the clothes Elyana had given him. She'd found them in an old white trunk that was so covered in dust that when she lifted the lid, all three of them coughed. Walker had no idea what to expect, but even he had to admit that the white silk tunic and pants were exceptionally well made and obviously expensive. He knew he ought to sleep, but he was overtired and his mind full of all that had happened.

Absently he wandered around the room, listening to the wind gust around the tower. He thought of how his dog, Blue, was always spooked by the wind, and a wave of homesickness washed over him. He wondered for the millionth time if he'd ever get home again. He wouldn't even mind being at the museum on the field trip that had started this whole thing, listening to boring old "Hoot Owl" Hamilton, his teacher, talking about stupid haystack paintings and the way that art dude Monet had captured the essence of light. Sighing, Walker stared down at the floor, realizing that he was standing on the mosaic of the dragon. He felt a tingle as he stood there, looking at the powerful creature frozen below him.

He bent and brushed some dust off the dragon. It was holding something in its claws, something in the very center of the circle—a square tile. Blowing the dust off that, he saw a strange triangular symbol. His eyes widened. It was the same symbol as the one on the door of the bones reader's house. What had Niko called it? The Dragon's Eye. Walker's heart began to beat faster. He wished Niko were here. He would know what this meant. The Dragon's Eye was flanked by square tiles marked with other symbols. One of them was the exact twin of his red charm. The realization was so surprising that his nose began to itch the way it did sometimes when he was concentrating. Could it be the key to something? he wondered. Was he supposed to see this mosaic? It couldn't just be a coincidence. He remembered Niko telling him that his master didn't believe in coincidence. He said all things happened for a reason. Right now, Walker, who had argued against such a nonlogical point of view, suddenly began to think that maybe, just maybe, Niko's master had been right.

Walker paced around the circle that enclosed the mosaic, his excitement growing. It was some kind of puzzle, he was sure of it—like a math problem. Surely these were the nine charms Niko was always talking about. There were nine square tiles spaced like the spokes on a wheel. He bent and cleaned them off one by one. Each revealed a circular stone of a different color—light blue, purple, green, black, red, yellow, pearly white, coral, dark blue.

Walker had no clue what they meant, but he knew that like in math, the first step was to write the problem down. He looked around the room for a piece of paper or something he could use instead, and a pen or a pencil, a stick of charcoal, anything to write with. But there was nothing, just dust and cobwebs galore, some brown things that looked an awful lot like mouse droppings, and all the white sheets.

There might be something under the sheets he could use, but for some reason he felt hesitant about pulling them off, as if he would be violating Elyana's trust or her mother's memory, or something. But he was definitely on to something, and he really had no choice. He reached out for the sheet closest to him and pulled. What he found surprised him so much that he exclaimed aloud. It wasn't furniture, as he had imagined. It was weapons—swords, lances, daggers. What would Elyana's mother have wanted with all these weapons? he wondered. He pulled off another sheet and then another. All arms, but no pen and paper. He'd have to improvise.

As his eyes scanned the room, they lighted on the trunk where Elyana had found the clothes, and he remembered seeing a stack of cut leather there. He hurried to the trunk, and sifted through the clothes until he found what he was looking for—a small square of tan leather about twelve by twelve inches. Then he selected a white dagger from one pile of weapons and sat down cross-legged next to the dragon mosaic. Slowly he carved a circle on the leather with the dagger, and then he started marking the sequence.

"Black," Walker whispered to himself before moving on to the next tile. "Green . . ." And the next, "blue . . ." And on until he'd carved all of them on the leather. His markings were crude but readable, and that was all that mattered. Carefully he folded the leather and shoved it into the pocket of his tunic. Exhausted, he lay down, feeling oddly satisfied with what he had done, and closing his eyes, he fell into a deep sleep, curled up next to the white dragon.

CHAPTER 10

Aurora heard a door swing open, and an icy blast of air hit her full in the face. She began to shiver uncontrollably, her arms and legs covered in goose bumps, her lips turning blue.

"Cold . . . cold . . . cold . . ." She repeated the word as if she were a small child reciting a lesson.

"Move!" one of the guards shouted, prodding her with the pommel of his sword.

Blindfolded, hands and feet shackled, Aurora shuffled out onto the freezing parapet. She had no idea whether it was day or night. The frozen stone stung her bare feet and with each step she could feel her flesh bond with the ice. If her body hadn't been so numb, she might have felt pain, but her capacity for feeling was long gone. They'd kept her without sleep for days now.

"That way!" said another Dragon, pushing her forward, his heavy fur cloak brushing the sleeve of her thin cotton dress. She remembered that she had a warm cloak too, somewhere back in the tower, back in the room she'd shared with Kite. It made her sick just thinking of the burning, evil glow of his yellow eyes after she'd sent out the charm. She had no idea who he really was, but he was someone of the dark, that much she knew for sure. Someone evil—more evil even than Lord Draco.

"Maybe we should hang her from one of the towers and leave her for the night birds," suggested the Dragon to her left with a harsh laugh. "She looks more like fodder than anything human should."

The other Dragon snickered in agreement. Suddenly, although there had been no sound of footsteps, Aurora could tell there was someone else on the parapet with them. She could also tell in her heightened state that the two Dragons who were guarding her didn't suspect the presence of this other person. She even knew who it was before he spoke.

"Maybe we should hang *you* from the wall instead, brother," Jah said in a voice as cold as the wind.

The two guards stopped walking and stood frozen on either side of Aurora. Neither said a word. And even though she was blindfolded, Aurora could see in her mind's eye Jah's red cloak with the black dragon embroidered on the back. An image flashed into her mind.

Jah is walking across a bed of fire at the House of the Black Rock as Lord Draco watches proudly. Jah looks younger, barely older than she is now. When Jah reaches the far side, Lord Draco unclasps a silver chain from around his neck and drapes it around the boy, the youngest page ever to undergo the Ceremony of the Five Fires and become a Dragon.

"Have you nothing to say, brothers?" Jah continued in the same cold voice.

Aurora didn't want to see, but the images kept coming. Jah's hand began moving beneath his robe, slowly but without hesitation. She saw that he was clutching something. The white dagger her mother had given to her brother, Kareem, and that had become hers after Kareem was kidnapped from the Gypsy camp, before he took the name Jah.

"Answer me," Jah said as he moved closer to the Dragon on her left.

But there was no answer, just the Dragon's quick intake of breath.

"Do you think this prisoner is here to amuse you?" Jah's voice was softer now, almost as if he had forgiven the two Dragons, who relaxed ever so slightly beside her, like rabbits who think the hawk has flown.

But Aurora could see what the Dragons could not—that Jah had removed the white dagger from his belt and was about to strike. She braced herself for the attack, but it never came. She could see in her mind that he was holding the dagger, staring at it, just as he had the night he had taken it from her. On the worn ivory handle of the dagger she saw something she had never noticed before—an image of a white dragon, very faint but there nonetheless. She suddenly knew that the white dragon was the secret of the dagger's power. It was a weapon with a will of its own—every time Jah would try to use it, it would stop him from doing so.

A hearty, mocking laugh from inside the tower suddenly broke the dagger's hold on Jah. More than that, Aurora sensed that the laughter upset Jah, made him intensely angry for some reason she could not understand.

"Follow me to the north tower! And bring *her*." Jah spat out the words as he pushed his way past.

Aurora felt herself being prodded along the icy walkway. Then she was picked up and carried up a steep flight of stairs. After a few minutes she heard the grating of metal on stone and then the creaking of a door. She sensed that they were entering a large room. It was hot, very hot. A fire was burning, its great flames giving off clouds of smoke.

"He actually began to laugh," a voice said, the tone incredulous.

"We were burning his eye out," said an[...] "And he started laughing."

The room was silent save for the popping of the[...] Then Aurora sensed Jah move forward toward some[...] one else, the source of the laughter. She could feel him standing over the person. Jah wasn't just angry, he was . . . Aurora didn't know how to describe what Jah felt, but somehow this stranger had defied Jah's sense of order, and he was determined to stamp it out, this defiance, no matter the cost.

"There is an arrogance about you, boy," rasped the voice of an old man in the tense silence, "that I have not seen in many, many years."

"There is an arrogance about you, old man, that I have not seen in many a prisoner," Jah retorted.

"The last time I encountered arrogance of this nature was in a student of mine," continued the old man in a mocking voice. "I believe you know him. He calls himself Lord Draco now, though when I knew him he had not the grandeur of such a title. Do you know, boy, what your lord believes?"

Aurora heard only silence punctuated by the hissing of the fire and the uneasy rustlings of the Dragons around her—except for Jah, who Aurora could sense was holding back all of the rage he felt inside.

"Lord Draco believes," the old man continued in the same half-mocking tone, "that he can release the n as Malachite from the cage in ...ped so long ago by the Lords of ... he will assume his true and terrible ... s to raise the black dragon, as Malachite has ... mind to believe he must. With the ... possession and allied with Malachite, Draco believes he will become all-powerful, his dominion extending from this world to all the worlds. However, he has chosen to forget that it was just such a desire for absolute power that brought down the last of the black dragon kings."

Aurora felt the tension inside Jah snap like a coiled spring. "Enough of this babble," he snarled.

"But there is one formidable obstacle standing in Draco's way," the old man continued, as if Jah had not spoken. "He does not know the pattern of the dragon that will unlock his dark desires. And do you know why that is amusing to me?"

Aurora hung on the old man's words, waiting to hear what he would say. But before the old man could reveal his secret, someone entered the room and whispered something to Jah which Aurora couldn't catch.

"To the Great Hall!" Jah commanded.

There was a scuffling of feet, and Aurora could feel movement all around her.

"Remember what your master seems to have forgotten," the old man rasped. "The smallest amount of light can defeat the greatest hordes of darkness."

"Everyone out!" Jah commanded.

"What about the girl?" asked one of Aurora's guards timidly.

Jah paused for a moment, then brushed past her. "Leave her with the old one. And take off her blindfold so that she can see the sort of fate that lies in store for her if she does not do as she is commanded."

One of the Dragons pulled off her blindfold as another pushed her farther into the room. She blinked in the sudden rush of light and heard the door close and the bolts locking into place.

"Come to me, Protector," the old man said, his voice weary but firm.

Aurora stumbled to her feet, squinting, but the light still blinded her.

"Not that way," he said.

It was an order, not a request. Instinctively she knew what he meant. Obediently she closed her eyes and began to breathe evenly, air in one nostril and out the other. She felt his mind open to hers, images flashing.

The Castle of the Seven Towers. Night. Niko entering a room filled with weapons. Choosing a silver sword with a

*gate engraved on the pommel and the nine charms hidden
inside. An old man with long white hair and a blue robe
with a hawk crest.*

Aurora stopped, her eyes popping open in shock.
"You're Lord Amber," she whispered. "We . . . Niko
and I . . . thought you were dead."

Lord Amber nodded. "We haven't much time, Protector, and what we have we must use wisely."

"How did you know I . . ." Aurora let her words
trail off.

But Lord Amber shook his head. "It is as obvious as
the color of your hair. The birthmark on your palm is
only for those who need confirmation of the ancient
prophecy. But you cannot help being who you are, just
as a scorpion cannot help its own nature, stinging those
that stand in its way."

Aurora hesitated for a moment. "I've done something terrible."

"What? Sent out a second charm?"

Aurora nodded, her eyes now used to the light, seeing the bleeding hole where Lord Amber's right eye had
once been. She gulped, unable to stop the heaving in her
stomach. "Your eye . . . ," she began, her voice filled
with horror at the sight.

"Don't trouble yourself about it. Now tell me, why
are you upset about the blue charm?"

"How did you know it was blue?"

Lord Amber brushed aside her question. "You sent forth a charm you believe to have been chosen by the dark. You are correct, for Malachite, who can assume any form, is indeed a dark sorcerer."

"You mean the boy in the cage was Malachite?"

"Yes, what did he tell you he was called—Kite?"

Aurora nodded. "So I failed again. Just as—"

"Silence!"

Aurora's mind reeled, for the word had not been shouted aloud but slammed into her brain. She shook her head as if to clear it.

"I'm sorry to resort to such tricks, but as I said, there is very little time. The battle between light and dark, good and evil, whatever you wish to call the dichotomy, is now upon us. If you know the prophecy, then you know that only the Circle of Three can possibly stop the black dragon and the destruction that is sure to follow should it rise."

"Circle of Three," Aurora whispered, a feeling of foreboding gripping her.

"Niko, the Chooser; Walker, the Bearer; and you, Aurora, the Protector. You must reclaim the charms or Lord Draco will use them to become the next black dragon king, and the evil Malachite will have his way."

Aurora frowned, thinking of the blue charm. "But there are only seven charms. The two Bearers each have one."

Lord Amber nodded. "As they should, according to the prophecy. So it is written:

> But if
> a second Bearer
> by the dark is then called forth,
> the black dragon shall be freed
> from its prison in the North.
> And the Bearer of the Dark
> shall face the Bearer of the Light.
> The white dragon must be risen
> or all shall be endless night."

"So by sending out the blue charm, I called forth this second Bearer," Aurora said, biting her lip.

"You did. This Bearer must come face to face with the other at a place where all nine charms converge."

"The North," Aurora murmured. "Here?"

Lord Amber nodded, his one eye studying her intently.

"Is there any chance that the prophecy could be wrong?" she asked.

"In small respects perhaps, but overall the Lords of Time were not wont to make many mistakes."

"You speak almost as if you knew them."

Lord Amber smiled and said nothing for so long that Aurora thought he wasn't going to answer. "You could say that Malachite and I both knew them, as well as we knew each other."

"But that's impossible. I mean, they lived so long ago. And Malachite is a dark sorcerer—"

"Who's to say what is impossible? Now the most important thing is for you to find Niko and the Bearer and to complete the circle. You must go quickly before Draco forces his way into your mind again."

Aurora felt her heart quicken at the memory of how Lord Draco had thrust himself into her mind. Her powers had not returned since that encounter—except for the way she'd been able to read Jah's mind. But that was more a symptom of their strange connection than any ability of hers, probably a result of the blood they shared by virtue of their births.

"You haven't lost your powers," Lord Amber said. "It's all about will. When your will is strong, so will your powers be. Now you must go."

"Come with me."

"No, child, my place is here. Let them think that I know how to place the charms in order to raise the black and white dragons. They will waste their time with me. Take heart, for you will not be alone. Along the way, you will be helped by the Thief."

"Thief?"

"He is one highly skilled in the art of evading capture, and it is his destiny to take the one thing you need more than any other. Now you must go."

"But what about my shackles?"

"Remove them."

"I can't."

Lord Amber raised a bushy white eyebrow.

"I can't do it." Aurora almost cried.

"Use your mind. Concentrate and will them to be undone."

Aurora closed her eyes and began to breathe the way the Old Ones had taught her, slow deep breaths, in one nostril and out the other. She concentrated on the shackles, on the way they bit into the skin of her wrists and her feet. In her mind she saw them opening and heard a grating sound. When she opened her eyes, she saw that they had loosened.

"Concentrate."

Aurora closed her eyes and willed the restraints to snap off, saw them springing open, saw herself free. And within a moment she was.

"Well done. Put on my fur cloak and these boots. They'll be too big, but they should at least keep you from freezing to death. Now unlock the door."

Aurora wrapped herself in the fur, slipped into the boots, and approached the door. She closed her eyes and began to breathe deeply once more, trying to concentrate, but in her mind she kept seeing visions of Lord Draco and his terrifying empty black eyes. She turned slowly.

"Can't you do it?" she asked Lord Amber.

"I could, but it is your destiny to walk through that door, not mine. You must go, Aurora, if only to prove to yourself that nothing is impossible, to believe what your grandmother, Titi, taught you so well. Hurry, Protector, for the others need you and soon it will be too late."

That did it. Aurora closed her eyes. She focused on the iron lock, on the big, rusty bolts that held the door shut. She thrust her mind at the bolts using every ounce of will she could muster, and to her surprise the door swung open.

 # CHAPTER II

A soft rustling woke Walker. He blinked, rubbing the sleep out of his eyes, and sat up slowly, staring at the secret door. Someone was out there.

He had gotten soundlessly to his feet when his eye was suddenly caught by the flames coming from the mouth of the white-dragon mosaic beneath him. Running through the flames, illuminated by the light from the window, was a column of symbols he hadn't noticed the night before. These were simple, crude shapes—a square, a star, a triangle, a cross, a semicircle, something that looked like an asterisk—and for some reason they seemed important, like a secret message meant for him. As he reached for the piece of leather on which he'd carved the charms, the door began to open.

He took one last look at the column of symbols and then quickly hunkered down behind the nearest sheet-covered pile, just as a figure in a dark, hooded cloak strode into the room. Walker barely had time to wonder who it was before the figure turned and he glimpsed violet eyes peering from under the hood. A cold prickling ran down his spine. It was Ikbar. And there could only be one reason he'd come here—to kill Walker.

Walker held his breath and watched Ikbar move toward the center of the room. He stopped by the dragon mosaic, but his body blocked out the light, so the column of crude symbols was no longer visible. Walker was relieved. Somehow, since Ikbar had the red charm, it seemed that the less he knew about the symbols the better. After a few minutes Ikbar glanced about, a strange smile creasing his pale, somber face. He murmured something Walker strained to catch. It sounded like "the ware of the white wagon. At last." Wagon ware? That made no sense. It had to be dragon. The hair of the white dragon? But dragons didn't have hair, they had scales. And why "at last"?

Ikbar turned just then, his eyes scanning Walker's side of the room. The trader's gaze stopped at his hiding place. One minute passed and then another. Walker could feel the sweat trickle down his back.

Finally, Ikbar looked away, moved toward the other

side of the room, and began throwing the sheets to the floor. Should he make a run for it? Walker wondered wildly. He glanced at the door. Escape was a long shot, but it seemed to be his only chance. As if he could hear Walker's thoughts, Ikbar turned and headed in Walker's direction. As he drew closer, running seemed like less and less of a good idea to Walker. He'd be out in the open, a moving target, and the trader had already demonstrated his talent with a knife. Yet if he stayed hidden, he was a sitting duck. Bang, bang, you're dead, he thought idiotically.

He tried to take a deep breath, willing himself to calm down. He had to do something. Action was key. Run for it, Crane, he told himself. Run or you're dead.

Ikbar came to a stop less than a foot away. Don't look over here, Walker prayed, clenching his teeth so tight he thought his jaw was going to break.

Ikbar muttered something under his breath and picked up an object from the floor. "Ahh," he murmured. "A dagger of the dragon."

Walker strained to see. It was the white dagger he'd used for carving the night before. He watched as Ikbar turned the dagger over. Walker noticed then the dragon carved on the dagger's white hilt. The man ran his hand over the hilt almost lovingly, then stashed the weapon out of sight beneath his cloak, and to Walker's utter relief, headed for the door. So Ikbar hadn't come here to kill him after all. He'd come all this way just to steal a weapon. Must be valuable.

Ikbar eased open the door and stepped through it. Just one more step and the door would close and Walker would be safe. He shifted his weight to ease the aching muscles in his calves. Ikbar was through the door now, his arm reaching back to pull it shut, when Walker's leg brushed against a sword, causing it to clatter to the floor. The clink of metal on stone echoed in his ears like a gunshot.

In a flash Ikbar was back inside and across the room. Walker sprang to his feet and tried to run but his legs were cramped, and before he could take more than a few awkward steps, Ikbar grabbed him by the loose cotton of his tunic.

"You little worm," he muttered as Walker struggled to free himself. "I should have killed you on the boat after you found that dream water."

"Leave me alone," Walker cried, trying to kick the cloaked man, but his arms were pinned behind his back and the trader managed easily to sidestep his clumsy moves.

"Before I end your useless life, I have some questions. Where did you get that charm?"

"I found it."

"Where?"

"In a fountain," Walker answered truthfully, remembering the class trip to the museum that had started this whole adventure.

"In this world?"

"I don't know what you mean."

"Allow me to refresh your memory."

Ikbar twisted Walker's arm so hard that the pain made him gasp.

"In which world did you find it?"

"Uh . . . I . . . uh . . ."

Ikbar yanked his arm once more, and this time Walker was sure he was going to break it.

"Which world?"

"My world," Walker cried out.

"Which one is that?"

"It's kind of like—"

But Walker never got to finish his sentence because he was interrupted by the sound of footsteps on stone just outside the door. Ikbar pushed Walker to the floor, out of sight behind a pile of linen, just as Elyana and Zoe walked through the secret door. With one hand around Walker's neck, he pulled out the knife Walker remembered from the boat.

"You make one sound and it'll be your last," he whispered as the cold metal of the blade grazed Walker's throat.

"Walker!" Elyana called softly.

Walker stared at the green silk of her dress, all he

could see of her through a gap in the sheets. Then he saw a flash of pink as Zoe came into view.

"Walker!" Zoe called more loudly. And then again, louder still.

Elyana called along with her, their two voices echoing in the silence. I'm over here! Walker cried silently as the trader tightened his grip on Walker's throat.

"Maybe he's still asleep," Elyana suggested.

The girls walked toward the center of the room, and Walker could see their faces for the first time. Elyana was looking back toward the door, but Zoe was turned in their direction, standing in a shaft of sunlight, dust motes dancing in the air around her. Please, please, please, Walker implored silently. See me. He stared hard at her through the gap, and slowly she turned until she was facing where he and Ikbar hid.

Ikbar's knife pricked the soft skin of Walker's throat.

Walker watched as Zoe's left eyebrow lifted slightly, as if she'd seen something. Maybe she'd caught a glimpse of their shadows. Or maybe she'd noticed the way the dust particles were swirling more frantically where he and the trader crouched. But just as his hopes rose, she turned and walked away.

"I don't think he's here," Zoe announced matter-of-factly. "He must have gone back to the boathouse."

What was she talking about? Walker thought wildly. He knew she'd seen something. I'm here! he wanted to yell, but the knife pressed to his throat took the words away.

"But he can't have left because he doesn't know the—"

"Come on, Elyana," Zoe insisted. "He's not here. You can see that for yourself."

"But he—"

"Really, cousin, let's go."

Come on, Zoe, Walker urged. Tell her. But instead, he heard the rustle of their dresses as the girls moved across the room, then the grating of stones as the door closed once more. One minute passed and then another. Come back! Walker implored, but he knew it was no use. They were gone. That stupid, rotten Zoe. She'd seen something, and all she had done was leave and take Elyana with her. Niko was right—maybe she did have it in for him.

After another minute Ikbar pushed off the sheet and yanked Walker roughly to his feet.

"Why did Elyana Summerwynd bring you here?" he hissed, his violet eyes intent on Walker's as he held the knife just inches from his throat.

"Because she likes me?"

"Don't play games with me, boy." Ikbar spat out the words as he flicked the blade closer to Walker's throat.

"Why don't you just kill me now and get it over with?"

"All in time," Ikbar replied. "But first you will tell me what I want to know. If you give me no more trouble, I will kill you quickly, sparing you pain. If you keep making me angry, I will kill you slowly so that the torture is excruciating. Am I clear?"

"Crystal," Walker mumbled.

"Tell me why she brought you here."

"She was trying to keep me safe."

"Why?"

"I don't know," Walker answered truthfully. "She's just nice, I guess. You know, some people are like that." He tried to keep the sarcasm out of his voice.

Ikbar nodded, as if satisfied with the answer. "Now tell me about your world."

"What about my world?" he asked, stalling for time, thinking of how his older brother, Bo, always said the best way to beat a bully who was bigger than you was to take advantage of the one thing you had on your side—the element of surprise. If you did something he wasn't ready for, then bam! you could bring down even a really big kid. Walker didn't think it would be so easy to surprise Ikbar, but it was just about his only shot.

"Well, it's kind of like this world. It's got mountains and rivers and—"

"Don't patronize me, boy. I want to know how you got from your world to this world. And don't go thinking your little friend will be coming to rescue you, either."

"What?" Walker burst out before he could stop himself.

Ikbar laughed, a harsh, hollow sound. "That's right. Your friend the Chooser is long gone from this world and you're on your own."

"I don't believe you."

"Suit yourself." The trader gave him a small, unfriendly smile. "Now tell me what I want to know before you no longer have a tongue to speak with."

Walker gulped, his mind racing, wondering if it was true that Niko was gone, but he made himself concentrate on what Ikbar wanted. "Well, I kind of closed my eyes and—"

"The charm. Tell me how you used the charm to get from your world to this world."

"It's kind of complicated," Walker began, knowing that the first step in getting the man off balance was to pretend to be cooperating. "So it may take some time. See, first you have to say some stuff in Latin. You know Latin?"

Ikbar shook his head. "No. What is Latin?"

"It's an ancient language from my world invented by these great warriors, the Romans, who built the Colosseum and conquered all these people, like the Greeks and the Carthaginians, and lots more. So you have to say these words and then—"

"What words?"

"Well, they're sort of difficult."

"Tell me."

Walker gulped, staring at the dagger, trying to remember something from Latin. He wished he hadn't failed the last test. "Words. Right. Okay, listen closely. *Puella puellarum amo amas etecetera etcetera agricola—*"

"Wait. Let me try it." Ikbar frowned, concentrating. *"Puella puellarum . . ."* He paused, chewing his lip as he thought, and in that split second Walker pushed him with all his strength. Caught off guard, the big man fell onto the pile of weapons, which clattered to the floor. Walker turned and started to run toward the door, but he wasn't even halfway across the room before Ikbar caught up and pulled him to the floor, his arms pinned above his head.

"That will cost you your hand," Ikbar growled, the knife blade flashing in the light. Walker tried to push him off, but it was like trying to bench-press a refrigerator, and Ikbar didn't loosen his hold in the slightest. Walker felt the cold of the metal touch his wrist, and he closed his eyes, waiting for the pain.

But it never came. Instead, there was a thud and the knife clattered to the floor.

"Get off him," Walker heard someone say. He opened his eyes to see Elyana holding a sword to the trader's throat.

Ikbar rose slowly.

"Elyana, how did you do that?" Zoe asked, her eyes wide with surprise.

"I don't know," Elyana answered hesitantly. "It was like I wasn't really doing it. It felt like someone else was inside my body, if that makes any sense."

"The last of the white dragons . . . ," Ikbar murmured under his breath so that only Walker heard.

"What did you say?" Elyana asked.

"I was just trying to protect you, Lady Elyana," Ikbar answered, bowing his head. "This boy is dangerous. He is the murderer all of Tyros is after."

"He is not a murderer," Elyana countered hotly. "And you know it."

"That's right," Walker echoed, scrambling to his feet. "*You* murdered Jek and the bones reader and took my charm. Now give it back."

"Yeah, where is the red charm?" Zoe demanded, as if, Walker thought afterward, she had a right to know. He was so preoccupied, though, that it didn't even occur to him to wonder how she knew it was red.

"Answer them," Elyana ordered, moving the edge of the sword closer to the trader's throat. "Do it for Taschen, the bones reader, because he was my friend."

"Lady Elyana," Ikbar began, fixing his violet gaze on Elyana. "Please, listen to me. This boy is lying to you. He is a danger and—"

"I mean it," Elyana insisted. "Why should I listen to

you anyway? Not only are you a murderer, but you're also a smuggler of dream water, something which, when my father learns of it, will be the end of you."

"It is not what you think."

"What I think is that you'd better answer them. Where is the red charm?" With that, Elyana grazed Ikbar's throat, leaving a jagged crimson line.

Zoe gasped, eyes wide, and Walker held his breath, wondering what Ikbar would do now.

"Come with me," Ikbar finally said. "But you must come alone, just the three of you, understand?"

They all nodded.

"I will take you to the charm."

And like the rats after the Pied Piper, they followed him from the room.

CHAPTER 12

The light flickered and then disappeared, obscured by the heavily falling snow. Aurora blinked the frost from her eyelashes and spotted the light again, a tiny yellow pinprick like a star. She shivered, huddling into the fur cloak Lord Amber had given her, and plodded down, lifting one frozen foot carefully after the other, making sure not to slip on the icy, snow-packed trail. She kept her eyes on the light, trying not to think about how cold she was and the enormity of the task in front of her. How she was going to find Niko, let alone get from the Cold Edge all the way back to the desert, then walk through a door in the air into another world, was a mystery she couldn't begin to unravel. But Lord Amber had said if her will was strong, nothing was impossible.

A mournful howling echoed off the cliffs. Aurora

froze as the wailing cries faded into the snow and the darkness. Wolves. Out in the night, hunting for food. She gulped and began to run. She'd heard of the fearsome blue wolves that still lurked in the Dark Peaks, bigger than regular wolves and twice as vicious. Those who believed the old stories said they were as smart as men because the blue wolves were once the companions of the Lords of Time. She hurried along the narrow path, thinking only of getting as far from the wolves as possible.

Suddenly she slipped and fell, sliding across the ice. A scream froze in her throat as she slid over the edge of the cliff, her hands slipping over the icy rocks. Down, down she fell—until her feet hit something hard. A ledge of rock. Breathing deeply, she collected herself and began the slow ascent back to the path. She pulled her body up a bit and then a bit more. Only a little farther to go. The cliff top was just out of reach. She stretched her arm up, reaching as far as she could, when the howling started again. This time it sounded even closer. Aurora gulped and reached upward for the next rock she could find. And the next and the next. She was almost there.

She stretched her arm up, grabbing on to a rock at the cliff top, when there was a sickening cracking sound. It was the rock. It was coming loose from the cliff. Only it wasn't a rock, it was an icicle. Her body swung wildly from side to side, her toes scrabbling for purchase. But the whole cliff here was ice. She was going to fall, crack her head open on a crag, and die in the Crystal Claw Mountains, alone. And no one would ever know.

Just then she felt herself being pulled upward in quick, jerky motions. She heard panting sounds from somewhere above her. She kicked her legs over the edge to safety, her breath ragged in her throat. And when she finally looked up to see who had rescued her, she was alone.

Aurora got up, listening, but there was no sound save the soft swish of snow from the sky. Maybe she'd dreamed the whole thing. She half feared that the magic of the mountains had seeped through her skin and was making her crazy—causing her to imagine things. She forced herself to continue along the path. She was concentrating so hard on the flickering light below that she didn't notice a light behind her until it was too late.

Arms grabbed her roughly from behind. She struggled to break free, but whoever held her was much bigger and stronger than she was.

"Let me go!" she shouted, her words snatched by the wind.

She twisted and turned, but whoever held her hung on tightly, managing to tie her wrists with thick, rough rope, and slide something wet and furry over her head—some kind of animal-skin sack that covered her from head to foot. Strong arms hoisted her up in the air as if she were a bag of grain, and she was carried onward. She didn't think her captor was a Dragon. There was something very un-Dragon-like about the furry bag and the grunts, something decidedly more primitive. A terrible thought struck Aurora. Maybe it was one of the Cold Edge folk. She'd seen them in the City of Sand and Stone, tall, silent people who dressed in furs and spoke a language of their own, people who didn't like the ways of the city. They had their own ways. Aurora gulped. Barbarian ways, some said, such as blood sacrifices to their gods in the form of children and animals.

Her thoughts ended when she was dropped unceremoniously onto a hard floor. She could feel the warmth of a fire before the bag was untied, then she blinked in the brightness of the firelight. The place was simple, with a desk in one corner, a table by the fire, and a doorway leading into another room. On the desk sat a large hunk of jacinth, the same gem that she'd seen in the ears of the Dragons, the one known to guard against magic.

"So this is what you have brought me? A Gypsy girl from the City of Sand and Stone or thereabouts. Isn't that right, girl?"

Aurora drew in her breath sharply as a woman appeared before her. She was small, with close-cropped black hair. Her skin was so pale it looked bloodless, and she had strange markings on her face, swirling circles in red, blue, and green. But it was her eyes that really bothered Aurora, large violet eyes that glittered like glass and stared as if looking right through her.

"I asked you a question. Are you from the City of Sand and Stone?" Her voice was smooth, almost musical, but its soft tones did nothing to hide the ferocity of those eyes.

Aurora nodded, deciding there was no point in lying.

"Stand up. Let me see you."

Aurora stumbled clumsily to her feet, her arms still tied awkwardly behind her.

"Untie her."

A man moved into the circle of firelight. His head was shaved and he was dressed in an animal skin. Aurora caught the purple gleam of jacinth in his ears. But most noticeable of all, on his left cheek was a purple tattoo.

"Thank you, Tybolt," the woman said after he had loosened the rope. Then she stepped toward Aurora, standing just inches from her, studying her as if she could look right into her heart.

"So what brings you to the Crystal Claw Mountains? You realize that most who journey here from your part of the world don't live to tell the tale."

Aurora nodded but didn't say anything.

"A silent one, are you? Well, we'll see about that." Aurora felt light-headed from the woman's scent, a combination of lavender and musky smoke. The woman raised her skeletal arms, and stretched out thin, white fingers. Even without physical contact Aurora could sense cold energy emanating from the woman, as sure as she could feel the melting snow dripping down her back.

Aurora couldn't help herself. She shivered.

A strange look came over the woman's face. Part surprise and part wariness. She took a step back and surveyed Aurora. "You have magic, but I cannot see what it is, where it is exactly. Perhaps . . ." She cocked her head to one side. "But it cannot be. At least, I never thought . . . Show me your palm."

Obediently, Aurora held up her left hand.

"No, your right."

Aurora slowly raised her right hand.

"The sign of the Dragon's Eye." The woman narrowed her horrible violet eyes and a strange smile crossed her pale lips. "So the Protector has come, as it was foretold."

"I don't know what you're talking about," Aurora mumbled. The door opened behind her, ushering in a blast of freezing air as another man entered, this one with a shaved head save for a long, black scalp lock. He was carrying a squirming fur bag over his shoulder.

"So many visitors," cooed the woman, turning her violet eyes to the bag. "Who have you found for me, Rigor?"

With a grunt, the man named Rigor thrust his bundle onto the floor. Out tumbled a boy dressed in a sodden wool cloak. He stumbled to his feet, blinking in the light. Aurora gasped. It was Serge, the boy with the moon-shaped scar from the City of Sand and Stone who had found her map.

"What are *you* doing here?" She blurted out the words without thinking.

"I will tell you exactly what he is doing here, Protector." The woman approached Serge and ran her fingers up and down in front of the boy, just as she had with Aurora. "He is following his heart on a quest for something he doesn't understand. He is, I suppose, the Thief."

"What?" Aurora sputtered. "But that's crazy. I mean . . ." She stared at Serge, who kept his eyes on his shoes. "You mean you really followed me all the way to—"

"However touching this may be," interrupted the woman, "there is business to be attended to. Now *you* have brought some magic, boy. Take off your cloak and turn around."

Serge swallowed and turned, shrugging his cloak to the floor.

"I don't know what you mean," he muttered.

"Ah, but I think you do." And before Aurora's startled eyes, the woman plucked the map of the Doors of the Hunab Ku from the back of Serge's pants.

He whirled around. "Hey, that's mine. You can't—"

But his words were cut short when Tybolt and Rigor each twisted one of Serge's arms until he cried out. The woman studied the map for a moment, then crossed the room to place it on her desk.

"Leave him alone!" Aurora yelled, rushing forward, but Tybolt reached out one of his massive tree-trunk arms and held her. She struggled but could not move forward.

"Let her go," Serge said, his dark eyes flashing. "And give me back that map."

"Why should I do that?" the woman asked, tapping one thin white finger against her porcelain temple. "Life is a bargain, you know, from the moment you're born to the moment you die. Each day is a deal struck with the maker to guarantee that you can live to the next."

"Who are you?" Aurora asked, staring at the tiny woman.

"A fair question," she answered, turning her strangely painted face to Aurora. "I am Lavandula, one of the Skyggni."

Aurora stared at her blankly.

"You have not heard of the Skyggni. No, we are a dying race and I am one of the few who remain. We are magic seekers, which is how I come to know of the prophecy. Whether I believe it or not, the book in which it is written is definitely a thing of magic."

"What prophecy?" Serge asked.

"Ask the Gypsy, for she has a large part in it, or so she believes, isn't that right, Protector?"

"I don't know what you mean."

"*Tsk-tsk*. You are not a very good liar, you know. But no matter. Suffice it to say that because there are those who believe that you are the Protector, they will pay me for you. And as the prophecy has two possible endings, depending upon who is victorious, that affords me a great deal of bargaining power."

With that she picked up a star-shaped box from her desk.

"As for you, boy, since life is a bargain, and as you have nothing to offer in exchange for your map, I have an idea." With the hint of a smile on her face, Lavandula reached for the box and pulled out a tile with a star on it, along with three small golden cups, which she placed before her.

"The tile will be hidden under a cup," she said. "If you guess under which cup, I will return the map and allow the two of you to go free. If you guess incorrectly . . ."

She stared hard at Serge. ". . . I take you on as a trader in magic and brand you with the purple serpent. Your possession of the map suggests that you would make an excellent magic trader." Then she shifted her piercing violet gaze to Aurora. "You I will sell to Lord Draco, who believes himself the heir to the black dragon throne. I am sure that for you no price is too dear, as he cannot afford for you to fall into the hands of the white dragon. Now, let the game begin."

Lavandula sank onto a puffy fur pillow and bobbed her head, indicating that Serge should sit opposite her. Aurora watched as Lavandula placed the tile under the middle cup.

"One chance," Lavandula said slowly, her purple gaze fixed on Serge. "One chance to decide your fate."

She flexed her thin, pale fingers over the cups and slid them around each other, slowly at first and then faster and faster, so that Aurora quickly lost track of which one concealed the tile. She glanced at Serge, whose dark eyes were intently studying the Skyggni's flashing fingers. After a few moments her fingers slowed, and the cups came to rest in a line across the table.

"Where is the tile now?" Lavandula asked, her violet eyes inscrutable as she gazed at Serge.

Serge bit his lip and slowly pointed his finger to the middle cup.

"Are you sure?"

Serge frowned and nodded.

Lavandula shrugged and picked up the cup. There was nothing there.

"You lose," Lavandula murmured softly.

"No!" Aurora screamed. "It's not fair! It was a trick!"

Calmly the Skyggni picked up the rightmost cup, revealing the tile. "We had a bargain," the Skyggni said in her soft voice. "Now you must live up to your end of it."

The two men advanced toward Serge. Their jacinth earrings gleamed in the firelight, and their serpent tattoos stood out, dark purple, the color of a bruise.

"I will mark you myself," Lavandula said. "I am good with a needle and will hurt you less than either of them, for their fingers are thick and they often slip. We wouldn't want to mar your pretty face, would we?"

"I will not allow this," Aurora cried, though no one in the room paid her any attention.

She closed her eyes and began her special breathing, concentrating on the two men.

"Tybolt, hold his arms. Rigor, his legs," Lavandula

commanded, as Aurora pushed her mind into the minds of the magic traders, willing them to stop.

"You may as well not waste your energy, Protector," Lavandula hissed. "This place and everything in it is protected against magic."

Aurora's eyes snapped open, and she found herself staring at the hunk of jacinth on the desk. So that's what Lavandula meant about the place being protected. Still, she might as well try. Hanging on to her concentration, Aurora shifted it to the bolts that locked the front door. Come on, she urged, willing the bolts to open, as they had at Nine Shadows Henge. But nothing happened. She closed her eyes again, pushing with that part of herself that had done it before, until a voice in her mind spoke to her, a voice she had never heard before, a calm, flat voice. *"Not now, Aurora. The Skyggni does not lie. Wait for the right moment. It will come."*

"Who are you?" Aurora asked aloud.

"I already told you," Lavandula said, "I am one of the Skyggni. Now sit down and don't interfere. If you do, your friend's face will be grossly disfigured. You wouldn't want that, would you?"

Aurora took a seat and watched as the struggling Serge was pushed to the floor. Lavandula pulled something from a shelf in the corner of the room, then glided over to him. She had an iron bowl in one hand and a small jar filled with purple ink in the other. She sank to her knees, placing the jar carefully beside her. The iron bowl she held up to Serge's face, as if judging the fit, and Aurora saw that it wasn't a bowl but a mask. In one side were tiny holes pierced in the shape of a snake.

"No!" Aurora whispered.

Lavandula slipped the iron mask over Serge's face. He thrashed around, trying to get his arms up, but Tybolt held him fast.

"Hold still," Lavandula murmured, "and the pain will be much less."

She took a needle she had fastened to her garment and dipped it in the purple liquid. With a small smile, as if savoring the moment, Lavandula held the needle over one of the mask's tiny holes.

"Leave me alone!" Serge yelled, struggling in vain. "You have no right to do this!"

"But I have," Lavandula replied calmly, relaxing her hand for a moment. "A bargain is a bargain. You are a man of honor, are you not? I won the game fair and square. Even you agreed to that. Now stop moving or the tattoo will not be perfect."

Serge lay still as the Skyggni's needle pierced his skin. Aurora watched as Serge was about to be branded a magic trader. She had to stop Lavandula, but how?

The voice in her mind spoke again. *"The time is coming. Wait and see. Then you will be able to act."*

Lavandula poked the needle through a second hole and then a third. As she dipped the needle in more ink, a bang and a muffled voice came from the next room.

"See who is at the back door," Lavandula ordered, nodding to Tybolt who hurried into the other room. After a moment gruff voices began to speak.

"I have been sent from Nine Shadows Henge."

"So?"

"You have something I must retrieve."

Oh, no, thought Aurora, a Dragon. She had to get out of here fast. If only Lavandula would leave the room.

"Close your eyes and pretend you are asleep," said the calm voice in her mind.

"Go, Rigor," Aurora heard the Skyggni say.

From beneath her eyelids Aurora could see the Skyggni wavering, not wanting to continue tattooing without her assistants. The voices beyond the door rose, clearly in argument. Aurora waited as the Skyggni studied her and then Serge. After an agonizing few seconds, Lavandula finally lifted off the mask and set it and the ink jar on the desk. She stuck the needle back in her dress. Then she too hurried from the room.

Aurora and Serge exchanged glances and then slowly got to their feet. A piece of wood fell softly into the fire at that moment, causing it to blaze, and in the flickering firelight something shiny caught Aurora's eye. A long silver sword. She knew that sword. It was Niko's, the one with the secret compartment in the hilt, the one where the charms had been hidden. She pointed to the sword and Serge nodded.

Aurora could hear the murmur of conversation from the other room, the Skyggni's high voice arguing with the deeper one of the Dragon. Aurora watched as Serge reached a hand up to his cheek. When he touched the three small purple dots, he winced.

It was now or never. Quickly, before she could lose her nerve, Aurora moved to the desk where Lavandula had put the map. She stuffed the parchment inside her cloak, then ran toward the window, motioning for Serge to get the sword and follow. Aurora reached to pull back the first bolt, and her stomach did a sickening flip-flop. It wasn't just bolted. The latch was frozen shut. They were losing precious seconds.

"Going somewhere?" The Skyggni's smooth voice cut through the air like a knife.

The heavy footsteps of Tybolt and Rigor thudded into the room. Aurora shot Serge a look of panic. Before she could think of what to do, Serge grabbed a stool and hurled it at the window. The glass shattered and Aurora dove through the jagged hole into the snowy night. The glass cut her face and hands, but she barely felt it as she struggled to her feet. And then Serge was behind her, pulling her up. She heard the rasp of bolts being drawn somewhere to their right, so they turned blindly to their left, staggering along in the snow. They began to run, slipping on the icy ground.

"There they go!" the Skyggni screeched.

Aurora turned to see yellow torches coming toward them. Tybolt and Rigor, accustomed to the snow and ice, moved quickly, gliding along the ground as if they were wearing skates. They would overtake her and Serge in moments.

"Hurry!" she urged Serge.

The two of them put on a burst of speed, and the Skyggni's house was out of sight. Another glance over her shoulder and Aurora could see their faces now, white in the glare of the torches. The magic traders would be upon them any second. A feeling of panic gripped Aurora. They were never going to make it. *"Now,"* urged the voice in her mind. *"Use your powers now. There is no magic to stop you here."*

Gasping, she stopped dead in her tracks and turned. "No, Aurora!" Serge cried as the burly men skidded to a halt in front of her. With no time to focus her breath, she simply concentrated on their eyes as they reached out to grab her, willing them to return to the house. She felt Serge come up behind her, but she shrugged him off, keeping her eyes fastened on the blank, empty eyes of the men. She forced her way into their minds, feeling her power growing. Their arms went slack at their sides and slowly they turned away.

"How did you do that?" Serge gasped, his eyes wide.

But there was no time to answer. "Run!" Aurora cried instead, afraid that the Dragon would be after them next.

Without a backward glance, she dashed through the snowy darkness. Serge slid along just behind her, the only sound their ragged breathing and the far-off howling of wolves.

CHAPTER 13

Zoe watched as Elyana trimmed the single sail of the small craft, trying to catch the slight breeze. But what little wind there was died as suddenly as it had sprung up, and the boat just floated in the still water. It reminded Zoe of the time she'd visited the bayous in Louisiana—the overgrown foliage, the stagnant water, the humidity rising and swirling around the boat. The water looked like boiling stew. No wonder Ikbar had hidden his ship here. They never would have been able to find it without the smuggler to lead the way.

"We're going to have to use the poles again," Elyana called, pushing a damp strand of hair out of her eyes as she smiled shyly at Walker and thrust a long pole into the water. Walker blushed as he picked up the other pole. Slowly the boat began to move once more.

Zoe sighed, looking from one to the other and rolling her eyes. This was no time for fun and games. Elyana herself had said Lost Swamp was a dangerous place where people simply disappeared. No way Zoe wanted to be anywhere near here at night.

She could not understand for the life of her what Elyana saw in a nerd like Walker. He was sort of cute, she supposed, but so immature and goofy, and here Elyana was this wealthy, beautiful girl who was engaged to a rich, powerful older man. How cool was that? Zoe shook her head. Even stranger, it seemed as if Elyana was actually enjoying this whole ridiculous adventure. Since meeting Walker, Elyana glowed and she looked even more beautiful than ever. Zoe didn't get the whole warrior-princess thing, either—the way Elyana had suddenly whipped out that sword back in the tower of the white dragon. Zoe had actually thought for a split second that Elyana was going to kill the smuggler. From the look in his eyes, he seemed to have thought so too. Who'd have expected that from her sweet, lovely "cousin"?

She cooled herself with the crude fan she'd fashioned out of reeds and stole a glance at Ikbar from beneath her eyelashes. It was her job, after all, to guard the prisoner on the way to his ship though with his hands and feet bound securely, there wasn't much he could do.

She was surprised and a bit embarrassed to find him staring at her with those weird violet eyes. He gave her the creeps. And then he smiled.

"What makes you so happy?" Zoe snapped.

"Whenever I see magic, I smile."

"What are you talking about?"

"The dream water in the right pocket of your dress is a very powerful thing. You should be warned that it could prove quite dangerous in the hands of one unschooled in its ways."

"What?" Zoe sputtered, her face reddening. How did Ikbar know about the dream water?

"And, of course, there's the charm," Ikbar said.

"But you said the red charm is on your boat." Zoe found herself whispering, although she and Ikbar were all the way in the bow of the boat, too far for Elyana and Walker to overhear them.

"I am not talking about the red charm, Bearer."

Zoe's eyes narrowed in suspicion. Just what was going on here? How did he know that she was a Bearer?

"Perhaps because you are from another world, you do not understand what it means to be descended from the Skyggni," Ikbar went on.

At his mention of her world, Zoe couldn't stop the shock from showing on her face. Watching her intently, he continued. "For that is what I am—a Skyggni, or magic hunter. There are only two of us left in all the worlds. We see magic, or more correctly, we feel it and are drawn to it."

Zoe frowned, that this man should know her secrets, but she was intrigued despite herself.

"Don't worry, Bearer. Your secret is safe with me. Let us not waste our time on trifles. I can see you are an intelligent girl with none of the childish idealism of the other Bearer, nor his blundering ignorance. I am sure you would agree that you cannot get something for nothing."

Zoe nodded. "I guess, but so what?"

"What I propose is an exchange—you help me to get free and I will make sure the other Bearer gives you what you want."

"What are you talking about?"

"The red charm. I know you want it, and I also know why. Or rather, why you think you want it. The Sisters of the Kuxan-Sunn, those malfeasant, interfering, dangerous sprites, are the ones who told you that you must get the red charm from the Bearer of the Light, isn't that correct?"

Zoe nodded before she could stop herself. She did need to get the red charm, but she also knew that it had to be given to her willingly by Walker.

"Once you have done so you are supposed to turn it over to them, and then you are free to go. They lied to you, however, for the Sisters rarely speak the whole truth. Did you wonder why they didn't want your charm? Someone with a quick brain such as yours undoubtedly jumped from that thought quickly to the next logical one—that once you gave them the red charm they would simply take your charm, too. And by the way—what guarantee did they give you that they would really send you home?"

Zoe was silent for a moment. The sound of bullfrogs croaking and the buzzing of insects through the swampy air was suddenly loud in her ears as she digested what Ikbar had said.

"Look over that way!" Elyana shouted, her voice breaking Zoe's troubled reverie. "The water flows more freely."

Zoe watched as Elyana and Walker hefted their poles, pushing again and again until the boat began to move toward the spot where Elyana had pointed, one which was less choked with reeds and the tall marsh grass that was impeding their progress.

"The Sisters told you nothing of the prophecy, I assume—nor of your role in it." He let his words trail off, his strange violet eyes fastened on Zoe.

She shrugged.

"There is a prophecy connected to the charms that can have two possible outcomes. You as the Bearer of the blue charm are integral to both; however, in one you are victorious and in the other you fail. The Sisters didn't tell you this because they want to control the outcome. There is too little time for me to give you more than the merest details, but in essence, to return balance to the worlds and restore everything to the way it should be, you must journey to Nine Shadows Henge, a place high in the mountains of the First World, from whence the charms came. There you must place the charms in a certain pattern.

"And you must not let Elyana out of your sight. She has already fallen prey to the Bearer of the red charm, but she must wed the heir to the black dragon throne for the blood of the white dragon runs through her veins. Only then will the black and the white dragons be united as they have been meant to be since the beginning of time. If you do that, the Dark Sorcerer will ensure that you return home."

Zoe was bursting with questions. "How will I get to this Nine Shadows place?"

"Agree to accompany Elyana there after she becomes engaged to Lord Draco, for it is his deepest desire that she see her future home as soon as possible. It is only appropriate, of course, that she be accompanied by her dear cousin."

"When?"

"I am not sure. It depends on when Lord Draco gets

to Tyros. Traveling from world to world is not an easy thing to do."

"Who is the Dark Sorcerer?"

Ikbar brushed her question aside with an impatient shake of his head. "That is something you cannot know just yet. Soon we will be upon my ship, and if you know anything about crews that trade in magic, you know that if they see that I am your prisoner, they will no longer serve me. If that happens, then I can no longer help you."

"So, I guess—" But before Zoe could finish her sentence, she was thrown to one side of the boat as the little craft suddenly caught the current and sailed deeper into the marshes.

"We did it, Zoe!" Elyana shouted, the wind whipping her hair about her face like a red veil.

Zoe smiled and got up, narrowing her eyes as she prepared to face Walker. "I'll be back," she murmured to Ikbar.

"We haven't much time." He spat out the words. "Many things rest on the outcome of your actions, Bearer of the Dark."

Zoe took a deep breath and moved toward Walker, who stood across from Elyana in the stern. Just before she reached him, she pretended to lose her balance and fell down, right at Walker's feet.

"Hey, watch out, Zoe!" Walker said, reaching out a hand to help her up.

"I have to talk to you," Zoe whispered in his ear. She cocked her head in Elyana's direction. "Just you and me."

Walker frowned, but he moved with Zoe toward the center of the boat. "Yeah?"

Zoe sighed deeply, then bit her lip so hard it brought tears to her eyes. She glanced up at Walker and said in the saddest voice she could muster, "I have to tell you something, but you can't tell anyone, not even Elyana. You promise?" Zoe paused dramatically, wiping her eyes.

Walker shrugged. "I guess."

"I'm not really Elyana's cousin. I'm a Bearer, just like you." With a dramatic flourish she pulled the charm from her pocket and held it up so that the blue stone caught the light. "We're from the same world, Walker, and I'm so scared now." She gestured behind her toward Ikbar. "We're both in danger, according to what Ikbar just told me."

Walker grimaced at the mention of Ikbar's name.

"I know he's a murderer and a smuggler and everything, but what he just told me I'm sure is true. Anyway, we've got to stick together or we'll never get home again." Zoe hid her face, and her shoulders shook as if she were sobbing.

"Hey, Zoe, don't cry. I just can't believe it. You, too?" He shook his head in surprise, his eyes straying to Elyana. "So Elyana has no idea?"

Zoe shook her head. "And I don't think we should tell her just yet. We wouldn't want to put her in any unnecessary danger."

"Why didn't you tell me before?"

"I never got the chance. All I know is that we've got to stick together if we ever want to get back to our world. We've got to trust each other." She gave Walker her most winning smile.

"Look over there!" Elyana suddenly shouted.

At first, Zoe didn't see anything, but then as she stared where Elyana was pointing she could just make out the dark outline of a large ship. It was covered in moss and blocked by the shadows of so many stunted swamp trees that unless you knew it was there, you would never notice it.

Carried by the current, Elyana's boat moved toward the larger ship. As they drew closer, the sunlight disappeared behind the dense canopy of vines that shrouded the area. No birds cried, no frogs croaked, and no mosquitoes whizzed through the air. But for some reason Zoe felt as if there were eyes watching them, hidden in the greenery. Walker returned to Elyana's side.

"It's really quiet," he said in a whisper, glancing

over his shoulder as if something were going to jump out and grab them.

"Yes," Elyana agreed softly. "It is a little too quiet."

"Maybe it's a trap," Walker said slowly.

"How can it be a trap?" Zoe retorted, not about to let Walker foil her plan. "No one knows we're coming."

"Still, I don't like this at all," Walker said. "We have no idea who's on that ship or how many of them there are."

Zoe allowed the silence to last for a full minute before she spoke. "I've got a plan."

"What is it?" Walker asked.

But Zoe didn't answer. She just proceeded to the bow and untied the ropes that bound Ikbar.

"Are you crazy?" Walker shouted. "What do you think you're doing?" He jumped up and headed toward the bow.

Zoe just smiled grimly. Ikbar in his dark cloak was like a shadow behind her. "Turn around," she ordered Walker.

"What?"

"See, my plan is very simple. We'll pretend you're Ikbar's prisoner. That way we can board the ship without any trouble."

Walker and Elyana exchanged looks but didn't say anything.

Then Zoe unsheathed one of the daggers they had brought from the tower of the white dragon. She hid it in the folds of her dress.

"I'll keep this right next to Ikbar, in case he tries anything. And Elyana can stay here and keep watch."

"What do you think, Elyana?" Walker asked.

Elyana's green eyes darkened with thought. "It might work."

"Well, do either of you have a better idea?"

Walker and Elyana both shook their heads.

"Okay," Walker said. "Let's try it." He put his arms behind his back and let Zoe bind them with the rope, but when she pulled out the rag they had used to gag Ikbar on their way to the harbor, he blanched. "Do you have to do that?"

"We have to make it look good."

"All right. I just hope this plan of yours works."

"Remember, Walker," she muttered under her breath, "we're in this together, like I said before. So don't worry, okay?"

He nodded with a resigned look in his blue eyes as the boat drifted closer to Ikbar's ship. It was anchored in a small cove, and they could see as they approached that vines and moss had been cut, gathered, and draped over the ship in order to camouflage it. It was so well hidden, in fact, that their boat almost smashed right into the prow.

"Say something!" Zoe commanded the Skyggni.

"What would you like me to say?" His tone was light, almost mocking.

She frowned, wondering why she had decided to trust him. She stood beside him, her fingers wrapped around the dagger in her dress. As Elyana guided the boat slowly alongside Ikbar's shrouded ship, there was no movement or sound from the deck above.

"Isn't it strange that the crew has not spotted us?" Elyana asked.

Ikbar shrugged but didn't answer, his eyes darting here and there as if he was looking for something.

"Ahoy!" Zoe shouted. She knew it was a pretty lame thing to say, but it was the only nautical word that came to her mind.

Still, there was no reply. There was just absolute, total silence. Dead silence, Zoe thought, and she shivered.

"What do you think happened to your crew?" Elyana asked. She was leaning on one long pole, her gaze calmly serious as she studied Ikbar. Her dress, Zoe saw in disgust, was muddy and soaked with sweat and dotted with grass stains, but Elyana appeared not to notice or even to care.

Ikbar didn't answer Elyana's question. She could see his eyes shifting from right to left, as if he was trying to spot something in the swamp. She wondered if trusting him had been a mistake. Well, if so, it was too late, because it was the only plan she had. Elyana poled the boat along until they found a rope ladder hanging from one side of the ship.

"Be careful," Elyana said, steadying the boat, her gaze lingering on the bound-and-gagged Walker. "This is a perfect place for snappers, you know. With their massive jaws, they can devour a grown man in one bite."

Zoe frowned in disgust. Better not think about that. With one heave she grabbed on to the ladder. Then she pulled herself up, followed by Walker, whom she pulled along behind her, and then Ikbar. Zoe scanned the deck, but there were no sounds and no movement. She spotted a hatch that rose up out of the center of the deck and pointed Walker toward it.

"Well, Captain," she announced, her voice loud in the stillness of the afternoon. "I'm sure your crew would like to know that you have captured the murderer whom everyone in Tyros is after, and that you are guaranteed to collect a big reward."

Walker glared at her, but she smiled sweetly. "I have to be convincing, you know," she murmured.

They made their way past the foremast and entered the hatch that led belowdecks. At the bottom of the few steep steps they found abandoned bunks and a table littered with half-eaten food but no crew. The place certainly looked abandoned, but Zoe had the strange feeling that there was someone there. She hoped Ikbar wasn't planning to double-cross her. She gripped the dagger more firmly.

Walker bumped her shoulder, motioning with his arms that he wanted to be set free.

"Since there's no one here, I guess it doesn't matter," Zoe said as she untied the rope around his wrists and pulled the gag from his mouth.

Walker rubbed his wrists where the rope had dug into his skin. Zoe could see in his eyes that he thought the ship was creepy too. Only Ikbar remained blank faced, apparently undisturbed by the sudden flight of his crew. Zoe didn't want to know why. She just wanted to get out of there—with the red charm, of course.

"Okay, where's the charm?" she asked, dramatically whipping out the dagger and pointing its sharp tip at Ikbar's chest.

"It's in my cabin."

"Then let's go get it," Walker said grimly.

They made their way up the steps. Ikbar motioned them toward a cabin at the rear of the ship. There they entered a small hallway with three doors.

"Which way?" Walker asked.

Ikbar pointed to the door straight ahead. Walker was about to push it open when Zoe suddenly grabbed his arm and yanked him back.

"Hey, what do you think you're doing?"

"He should go first," Zoe said, prodding Ikbar. "Just in case the place is booby-trapped."

"Good thinking," Walker agreed as he and Zoe followed Ikbar into the room.

They stopped and started in surprise. The place was in shambles. Papers and charts were strewn across the floor with books and vases and instruments made of glass and silver that Zoe had never seen the likes of before. Drawers were pulled out, their contents spilling every which way.

"Looks like we're not the first to get here," Walker said slowly, moving toward the small round window that overlooked the rudders. "Where is the charm?"

Ikbar searched the mess on the floor. Calmly he bent and picked up the fragments of a beautiful cut-crystal vase. "It was in here. Whoever did this must have it now."

Zoe glanced at Ikbar's pale expressionless face, and a quick flicker in those violet eyes made her know with certainty that he was lying. The little worm, she thought, pursing her lips. He was trying to double-cross her. But then she got an idea.

"Well, I guess there's nothing more to do here," she said, staring at Walker. "We might as well just torch the ship."

"What are you talking about?" Walker blurted out.

Zoe clenched her teeth. He really was a fool. "You

know," she said slowly, raising her eyebrows as a signal to Walker. "This ship is of no further use to us now, so let's torch the heap of junk."

Walker's eyes lit up as he finally understood. He reached for the flaming stick dipped in tar that was burning in a sconce on the wall.

"I'll start with the bow," Walker announced, making as if to leave the room.

"You're insane," Ikbar barked. "Both of you. But you wouldn't dare. Even your stupidity must know some bounds."

"Oh, yeah?" Zoe burst out, grabbing the torch from Walker's hand and lighting some of the papers that littered the floor. They caught instantly, the yellow flames bright in the dim room. Zoe watched Ikbar, noting how his eyes darted to the left side of the cabin. She moved that way, lighting a few more papers as she went.

"Is there not some kind of deal we can make?" Ikbar asked in the same expressionless tone of voice. But Zoe thought she caught a hint of anxiety in it.

"Well, since you don't have what we want," she countered quickly, "I don't know how we can make a deal. Isn't that right, Walker?" She threw the torch to Walker, who caught it in one hand.

"I'll go below and set the cargo on fire," Walker said.

"You'll kill us, fool!" Ikbar shouted, all pretense of calm deserting him.

Walker proceeded toward the door as the fire began to spread through the room. Zoe stared at it uneasily. She hoped she hadn't gone too far. But just then Ikbar spoke, the sweat dripping down his pale face. "I will give you the charm as you wish, but you must put out the fire."

Ikbar headed to the left side of the cabin and lifted one of the floorboards, revealing a hidden compartment. He reached inside and pulled out a small wooden box, which he tossed to Zoe. Inside, just as she had hoped, was the charm, gleaming a rich ruby red.

"Walker, I've got it!" she shouted. "Here!" She tossed it to him, just as something crashed into the ship. The impact sent them all flying to the floor.

"Prepare to be boarded!" boomed a voice from somewhere outside. "We know the boy murderer is here. So come out one at a time, with your hands raised."

"No, Captain," shrieked Elyana. "Walker is innocent." But the captain must not have paid her any attention because next came the thudding of feet on the deck.

"It looks as if your time is up, fool," Ikbar hissed, with a satisfied glance at Walker.

Walker looked at Zoe with panic in his eyes.

"Give me the charm," Zoe whispered. "It'll be safer with me, just in case something happens."

Walker hesitated for a moment. Neither noticed Ikbar slipping out of the room.

"We've got to trust each other, Walker," Zoe insisted. "I mean, we're each other's only hope if we ever want to get home again."

Footsteps pounded just outside. "I guess you're right," Walker said. He held the charm for a few more seconds and then slowly handed it to Zoe.

Just as Zoe placed the charm in a small pouch in the folds of her dress, soldiers burst into the room. They grabbed Walker and pushed him to the floor.

"At last I've finally caught you." It was the same captain who had been searching for him the night before. He stood in the doorway, his gold-ribbed tunic and golden sword gleaming in the torchlight. "We were in the swamp investigating this strange ship when you appeared. I suspected you had convinced the trusting Elyana to hide you."

"Hey, leave me alone! I'm innocent! I'm telling you, you've got the wrong guy!" Walker managed to gasp as one soldier banged his head against the wood. "Tell them, Zoe!"

"It was terrible." Zoe choked out the words in the most dramatic voice she could muster. "He threatened to kill me if I didn't do what he wanted."

"You're safe now, my lady."

"I didn't do anything!" Walker cried out as they pulled him to his feet, binding his arms and legs in shackles. "Ikbar did. Tell them, Zoe."

"There's no one else here," said one soldier. "The murderer lies."

"But there was. Tell them, Zoe," Walker implored. "Tell them how he tried to kill me and—"

"Silence boy. Allow the lady to speak."

Quiet descended on the little room and all eyes were on Zoe. "I don't know anything about someone named Ikbar," Zoe said in her sweetest little-girl voice. "I was just so frightened." She covered her face with her hands, as if she were sobbing.

"What?" Walker exploded. "She's lying!"

"Shut up," a soldier yelled, punching Walker in the gut. The boy grunted once and lay still. Zoe stole a glance at him from between her fingers. There was a dazed look in his eyes as he glared at her, but she could see anger, too. She felt a little bad but, well, the whole thing had been a game, hadn't it? And she couldn't help if she was the winner, although she did wonder how Ikbar had made himself disappear like that. Maybe it had something to do with being—what did he call it—a magic hunter.

The captain pulled out a scroll and began to read. "In the name of the council of traders of the city of Tyros, the boy known by the name of Walker is hereby charged with the murder of two men in cold blood."

CHAPTER 14

Zoe paced from one end of the black-and-white-striped fur rug to the other, chewing on a fingernail the way she always did when she was thinking. She stopped at the elegantly carved wood and marble dresser. Although Zoe had never seen anything as exquisitely made, it wasn't the dresser that interested her. It was the small bottle she'd placed on top. The moonlight slanting in through the long windows fell on the blue-tinted glass and created a dancing pattern of light in the room. She stared entranced, watching the light swirl, now silver, now gold. She had to force herself to tear her eyes away. If she went ahead with her plan, she would have to be very careful when she opened the bottle of dream water.

She turned and paced once more, stopping this

time in front of a gilded full-length mirror. Idly, she studied her reflection, smoothing a wrinkle out of the periwinkle blue silk nightdress she'd found in Zecropia Palmata's trunk, marveling at the softness of the fabric and the way it fell in luxurious folds to the floor. She turned and walked back slowly toward the dresser, her eyes on the little bottle. If she was going to do it, tonight was the night.

Without another thought, Zoe approached the massive four-poster bed and pulled the long silk cord. She sighed and smiled ruefully. What she was planning to do was for Elyana's own good in the long run. On top of that, it was the only way she knew to make sure that she could finally go back to her world.

"Come in," Zoe said when she heard a gentle knock on her door.

Sela opened the door, her dark head bowed as she entered the room. Zoe loved the way the servant totally deferred to her, as if Zoe were royalty or something. Too bad maids in her world didn't act like that.

"Is Elyana still awake?" Zoe asked.

"Yes, miss," Sela answered softly. "I heard her crying on my way here. I think she is upset about the trial to—"

"That's enough, Sela," Zoe interrupted. "Lady Elyana's thoughts are not yours to consider. I believe you are forgetting your place, something I would hate to mention to Master Summerwynd. Now bring me a pitcher of lemon water and two dark blue crystal glasses and meet me in Elyana's room."

Sela nodded, a flush suffusing her cheeks, and quickly scurried out of the room. Zoe smiled. The maid was totally afraid of her. Perfect.

Zoe pulled a matching dressing gown over her nightdress and thought about her plan. She remembered that drippy Niko saying that if the dream water was diluted and someone drank it, then that person would in a very short period of time begin to lose their will. They would forget the little details of their life and become mindless, directionless, without a thought in their head, easily controlled. That was perfect for what she needed Elyana to do. Zoe'd just have to make sure that she gave her cousin regular doses of the stuff to get her through the trial tomorrow, then the ordeal of meeting her fiancé, and after that the trip to the other world to see her new home. Niko had said a few drops were enough. But what did that mean? Two? Three? And in how much water? She wouldn't want to overdo it. The results could be disastrous.

Even more important, though, she would have to be very careful when she opened the bottle. The temptation to touch the dream water was so great. In fact, she realized with a shiver, she was holding the bottle in her hand again, although she didn't remember picking it up. It took all her willpower not to open it immediately.

Quickly she shoved the bottle into the pocket of her robe. Then, before she could lose her nerve, she headed down the hall to Elyana's room. She knocked once softly and opened Elyana's door without waiting for a reply. The suite of rooms was huge —it was almost the size of her mother's entire house back in her world— and Elyana was nowhere in sight. For a minute Zoe worried that the stupid girl had gone ahead with her ridiculous plan to try and sneak Walker out of prison, but then she heard a noise behind the closet door.

"Elyana?" Zoe said.

"I'll be with you in a moment," Elyana called from inside the closet.

There was a gentle rap at the door and Sela entered, carrying a silver tray.

"Bring the tray over here," Zoe ordered. "And put it on the table."

The maid hurried over and carefully placed the tray on the low stone table.

"Go now," she growled at the poor blushing maid. Sela bowed and almost ran out of the room. If the situation hadn't been so grave, Zoe might have laughed. As it was, she knew she had not a moment to waste.

"I've brought you some lemon water," Zoe called to Elyana. "I thought you might find it soothing."

"I'll be right out!" Elyana called. "And I'll tell you my plan."

Plan? thought Zoe. So Elyana was back on the idea of springing Walker. Clearly, she hadn't come a moment too soon. Carefully, her eyes on the closet door, she removed the small glass bottle from her pocket and placed it on the tray.

"I will not touch or smell the dream water," she murmured to herself. "I will not touch or smell the dream water." She repeated the words as if they were a mantra. Picking up the bottle, she gently broke the thin silver seal. Then she pulled off the stopper. A multicolored light swirled out of the bottle, rising before Zoe like smoke from burning incense. Zoe could almost hear a voice whispering to her, but it wasn't speaking in words. It was more like music—beautiful, strangely familiar music.

"I will not touch or smell the dream water," Zoe repeated stubbornly as the enticing scent wafted around her.

"What did you say?" Elyana asked.

Zoe started in surprise and blocked the tray with her body. She stared at Elyana, who was dressed all in black.

"Uh . . . nothing," Zoe replied quickly. "What are you doing?"

"I'm going to try and save Walker. I couldn't live with myself if I didn't at least try. Will you help me black my face?" She indicated a tin of black goop in her hand.

"Sure," Zoe said, inwardly cursing herself for having missed her chance with the dream water. Now what was she going to do?

"Oh, wait. I forgot a cloth. I'll be right back," Elyana said and ducked back into the closet.

Perfect, Zoe thought. Quickly she poured lemon water into Elyana's goblet. Then she added one drop of dream water. And another. She watched as the liquid bubbled for a moment. Then, as she heard Elyana leaving the closet, she added one more for good luck and quickly replaced the stopper. She put the bottle in her pocket just as Elyana sat down in the chair opposite.

"I know you think I'm crazy," Elyana said, "but I have to do this . . . alone. You've already done enough. More than enough. It's not your fault that the captain wouldn't believe you that Walker was innocent. It's not right for you to endanger yourself anymore because of me."

Zoe smiled her most endearing, sympathetic smile, the one that always worked on both her parents when she was trying to wheedle her way out of trouble. Lucky for her, Elyana was so trusting, she never doubted Zoe hadn't defended Walker. If she only knew that Zoe was the one who'd sealed his most unfortunate fate. "Elyana, you're upset. You're not thinking clearly. Have some lemon water and let's talk about this calmly and rationally. You said yourself that the hanging stones never lie and Walker will be found innocent." The whole idea of some stones determining guilt or innocence in a murder case struck Zoe as completely barbaric—she didn't even begin to understand how it worked. Elyana said the system was as old as the city of Tyros, a law that even the rational magic-hater, Lyonel Summerwynd, couldn't change.

"I feel calmer than I have all night. Really. I know this is the right thing to do. Just like I know I can't marry Lord Draco, even though my father wishes it, and that I should not go to his palace in the North, as it is not my destiny. Thank you, though, for offering to accompany me. That was so sweet of you."

"Have a drink first," Zoe insisted, pushing the goblet toward Elyana.

"I should really just go. Before I lose my nerve."

Elyana stared at the goblet for a moment. Zoe was holding her breath, waiting, when she suddenly had an idea.

"I know," Zoe said brightly. "Let's drink to your success rescuing Walker."

Elyana smiled. "Good idea."

Both girls picked up their cups. Zoe watched in anticipation as Elyana slowly took a small sip.

"It tastes different than usual. Sweeter somehow or maybe spicier, I can't tell which."

Zoe sipped hers. "Tastes the same to me."

Elyana took another sip, then rose to her feet. "I have to go now before—" Suddenly she slumped backward into her chair. Her body went rigid and her eyes rolled back in her head.

"Oh, no!" Zoe gasped. She'd used too much and the dream water had killed Elyana. But then the girl's eyes slowly opened, and she shook her head as if to clear it. She sat up and straightened her shoulders as if nothing at all had happened. But her eyes told a different story. They were blank and empty.

"Where did you say you have to go, Elyana?" Zoe asked.

"Do I have to go somewhere?" Elyana replied, her voice soft and vague as she fingered her black cape with a look of confusion on her face. "Why am I wearing this cape?"

"I don't know," Zoe said. "I think you should put on your nightdress and go to bed."

"Yes," Elyana agreed.

"We have a big day tomorrow."

"We do?"

"Yes. Don't you remember what's happening tomorrow?"

Elyana shook her head slowly, biting her lip like a

small child trying to think of the answer to a teacher's question.

"The trial of the boy who murdered the man on your father's ship. The whole city of Tyros will see him brought to justice tomorrow."

Elyana nodded slowly. "The stones never lie."

"That's right," Zoe agreed. "They never do."

After Elyana was safely tucked in bed, Zoe returned to her own room. With a sigh of satisfaction she took the bottle of dream water out of her pocket and carefully hid it in the bottom drawer of her dresser. Then she stretched and yawned. Things had gone even better than she had anticipated.

"Brava," said a soft, tinkling voice behind Zoe.

She jumped and turned to find herself facing Mynerva, the littlest Sister of the Kuxan-Sunn. Next to her stood Ijada, the eldest. Both of them smiled at Zoe, their sapphire blue eyes fastened on her hungrily, their blue green dresses shimmering with that strange, unearthly glow.

"You truly are a massster of the dark," Mynerva said with a tinkling laugh.

"What are you talking about?"

"Come now, Zoe," Ijada said in her soothing, musical voice. "That was wonderful to watch. Very good work for sssomeone so young and untrained."

"I don't know what you mean." Zoe's heart was

beating fast. She didn't trust these Sisters after what Ikbar had told her.

"Now that you have so beautifully accomplished what we asssked you to do, it is time for you to give usss the red charm."

"I see," Zoe said slowly. "You want me to give you the red charm. And then what exactly are you going to do for me?"

Neither Sister said a word as they watched Zoe move around to the other side of the bed.

"What will you give me?" Zoe asked again. "A false promise to go home?"

Ijada and Mynerva looked at each other.

"What do you mean?" Ijada asked. "Give usss the red charm and then you can go home."

"Well, maybe I don't want to go home anymore. Or maybe I don't believe it's in your power to send me home at all. See, I'm not as stupid as you think, just because I don't have the kind of weird powers you do and because I'm from a different world. Let's just say I know about the prophecy and my role in it, and I know just who it is I'm supposed to give the red charm to and it's not you, ladies."

"Foolish girl. A little knowledge is a dangerousss thing, for you have no idea of the true implications of the prophecy. Clearly you have never met the likes of Lord Draco, let alone come in contact with the power of the black dragon and the Dark Sorcerer. The truth is, we are sssimply trying to protect you."

"So I'm supposed to believe that all you have at heart is my well-being? Well, I'll tell you right now you're lying, and I know you are, even if you're not human, because you're doing exactly what humans do when they lie."

"What is that?"

"Using the word 'truth.' It's a dead giveaway."

Ijada's blue eyes narrowed and darkened to a steel gray, like the sky before a storm. "You may think you are being clever, but your very life hangs in the balance. Give usss the charm, and we will make sure that you will live to return home to your world."

"To your friends, Jen and Ashley, to your father whom you love more than anything, and to Shane, the boy of your dreams," Mynerva added, gliding silently over to Zoe.

Zoe bit her lip, unable to stop herself from thinking of her father and Shane. She felt confused all of a sudden. Maybe the Sisters were speaking the truth and it would be better to listen to them.

"Come, Zoe, give usss the charm," Mynerva crooned in an entrancing singsong that suddenly reminded Zoe of the voice of the dream water.

"Give usss the charm," Ijada echoed.

Zoe shook her head, but she could feel herself weakening.

"Shane will be yours," Mynerva crooned.

Zoe reached into her right pocket and closed her hand over the smooth, cold shape of the red charm.

"Give usss the charm," sang both Sisters, floating ever closer, their blue green dresses shimmering in the torchlight.

It was so tempting just to give in to them and do what they wished, but hadn't listening to Ikbar actually gotten her the red charm? That thought settled it for her.

"No," Zoe said suddenly, breaking the spell the Sisters were trying to cast on her.

"How dare you defy the Sisters of the Kuxan-Sunn!" Ijada exclaimed. Her blue eyes narrowed and flashed sparks into the dimness of the room. "Do you know what we can do to you?"

"No," Zoe said, making sure her voice sounded calmer than she felt. "All I know is that I've got the red charm and you don't and there's not a single thing you can do about it."

"You shall pay for this," Ijada hissed. "You shall see jussst what happens to those who defy the Sisters of the Kuxan-Sunn." Then with a swirl of green light the Sisters disappeared, leaving Zoe alone in the darkness.

CHAPTER 15

The sun beat down on Walker as the cart moved slowly up the narrow stone road that led out of the city. He swallowed but his mouth was as dry as the barren land around him. He hadn't had any food or water for an entire day. Not that he was hungry. He was too anxious to be hungry. His life hung in the balance, all to be decided by some stone. It was too stupid for words.

Walker peered through the bars of the cage in which he was imprisoned. Ahead and behind him marched imperial guards dressed in the crimson and gold of their regiment, all marked with the lion crest of Tyros.

"Where are you taking me?" Walker asked for the hundredth time.

As before, no one answered. No one turned. No one did anything but continue to march. For the millionth time he cursed himself for not listening to Niko, for trusting Zoe, and worst of all, for giving her the red charm. If only . . . but there was no time left for "if only's"—it was already much too late for that.

He sighed again as they crested the hill. Walker saw a crude stone amphitheater rising before them. And he could hear the muffled roar of what sounded like hundreds, maybe thousands of people. As the procession approached, a small crowd began to gather.

"Murderer!" someone shouted.

Other voices took up the chant. "Murderer! Murderer!" Horror washed over Walker as he saw the hate contorting people's features. The crowd surged toward him, and if his captors hadn't drawn their swords to shield him, it might have all been over for him right then.

An iron gate rose with a thunderous grating, and Walker's procession moved forward into a dark stone hallway under the seats which rose above. From above and behind him, he could hear the crowd's cries for blood.

He was led into a circular arena surrounded by hundreds of seats. One huge, gnarled tree, its green, leafy branches reaching up into the sky, its trunk so broad it would have taken ten large men linking arms to circle it, was the only prop on this horrible stage.

A large gray stone with a hole in the middle

hung from a vine that was tied to a branch about fifty feet from the ground. Below the stone, on three massive sections of tree trunk, were three more stones, each the size of a man's head: one gold, one silver, and one black.

The hanging stones.

A soldier unlocked Walker's cage and another grabbed him and threw him to the ground in the center of the arena. When Walker looked up at the rows and rows of spectators, the scene was as chaotic as a Lakers' game when the fans didn't like the ref's call. Trumpets sounded and the crowd went silent as a man with a shock of steel gray hair and wearing a crimson and gold mantle entered a special section directly across from Walker which was shaded by a crimson-and-gold-striped canopy. It was Lyonel Summerwynd. Behind him Walker could just make out the fiery-tressed Elyana and beside her, the dark-haired Zoe. Walker gritted his teeth as he stared at Zoe, anger surging through his veins like fire.

Lyonel Summerwynd bowed to the crowd, inclining his head from one section of the amphitheater to the other, smiling as the people applauded.

"Today we have gathered so that the ancient oracle of Tyre can determine the guilt or innocence of this boy, who has been accused of not one but two murders in our great city of Tyros."

Lyonel paused as the amphitheater swelled with the catcalls of the crowd. Walker took a deep breath, trying to quell the sick feeling in his stomach. He tried to catch Elyana's eye, but there was something wrong. It was as if she'd never seen him before. Her face was blank and she was slumped back in her seat, as if she were too tired to be bothered with the proceedings. Or as if she wasn't even aware of what was going on. She looked lifeless, mindless, almost unconscious. Like a zombie. Zoe caught Walker's gaze and wrapped her arm protectively around Elyana, pulling the listless girl toward her. Zoe had no trouble returning Walker's gaze, her light blue eyes cold like ice.

"As the people of Tyros know, the ancient oracle of the gods does not lie. If the golden stone is the one, then the boy is innocent. If the black stone, then his guilt or innocence cannot be determined. But if the silver stone is the one, then the boy shall be found guilty and he shall be stoned to death."

A great roar rose from the crowd, and fists brandishing rocks swept in a horrible wave across the amphitheater. Walker gulped but couldn't swallow as he studied the seething crowd, all itching to kill him.

"May justice be served!" Lyonel Summerwynd boomed as he looked down on Walker and raised his right hand.

At this signal, the guards moved swiftly into position

around the perimeter of the amphitheater, leaving Walker alone beneath the great, gnarled tree. A hush descended on the crowd as a hooded figure stepped out of the center archway into the arena. He carried a flaming torch, and as the crowd watched breathlessly, he lit a fire under the gray stone. Smoke billowed thickly toward the sky, dancing around the gray stone, as a musky odor filled the air.

The hooded figure turned to Walker, his face shrouded so that only his dark eyes were visible. "What say you?"

Walker stared at the figure in uncomprehending panic. He had no idea what he was supposed to say or do.

"What say you?" the shrill voice repeated.

Walker stared blankly, the sudden silence ringing in his ears as the spectators all waited expectantly for him to speak.

"He says guilty," a voice called out from the stands.

Walker swallowed and protested as loudly as he could, "No! I'm innocent!"

The crowd roared their disapproval, but the hooded figure silenced them with a wave of his small, pale hand. He closed his eyes and began to chant:

> "Stone of Tyre, Stone of Tyre,
> Speak he truth, or be he liar?

Shall he live or shall he die?
Speak now stones that never lie!"

The hooded figure nodded his head once, and three guards stepped forward and took hold of the gray hanging stone. With a great heave they pushed it over to the circle of guards surrounding Walker, who passed it around, faster and faster, until the stone was spinning by itself. Chanting still, the group took a few steps back.

Walker's eyes were riveted on the stone as it spun past the gold, the silver, the black. And again, gold, silver, black. Hoping against hope, he stared at the gold stone. It had to be the gold stone. He was innocent after all, and even Elyana had said the stones never lied. Gold, silver, black, the hanging stone continued to spin as the crowd gazed raptly at it.

Just as it began to slow, teetering past the silver, the black, and heading for the gold stone, a flash of green light, imperceptible to all but Walker, altered its course. A soft voice hissed in his ears, "I told you that one day you would be sssorry," and Walker saw the glowing green form of Mynerva, the littlest Sister of the Kuxan-Sunn, to whom he had sworn he would never give the red charm. He knew then, although he couldn't have said exactly how, that the red charm, his charm, had not been responsible for opening the door that had brought him to this world as he had supposed. It had been the dark magic of the Sisters, although why, Walker did not know.

Finally, the hanging stone knocked into the silver stone, which tumbled to the ground. The people rose to their feet, screaming and yelling, rocks in their hands, ready to pelt him, ready to watch him die.

The hooded figure raised both arms to the crowd. "The ancient oracle of Tyros has spoken. The boy has been found guilty and shall be stoned to death."

"Wait!" Walker cried, but no one heard him.

He looked around frantically for a way to escape, but there were guards blocking every exit. The throng began surging from the stands, when suddenly a commanding voice that seemed to penetrate every inch of the amphitheater cried out, "Stop!"

Walker started in surprise as a hush fell over the crowd. The guards in the arena parted to allow a figure dressed in a bloodred robe to approach the hanging stones. He was flanked by other figures similarly garbed and carrying long swords. Walker's mouth froze in an *O* of horror as he stared at the cold, impassive face that he knew only too well. It was Lord Draco of the House of the Black Rock.

"As you may or may not know, I am about to become officially betrothed to Elyana Summerwynd, the daughter of the honorable praefectus regis of Tyros," Lord Draco thundered.

Walker stared at Elyana, who remained as blank-faced as before. This was the person Elyana was supposed to marry?

"And as you also know, it is my right as her betrothed to ask her father for a gift of my choosing." Lord Draco turned to Lyonel Summerwynd, his sharp, craggy features expressionless. "And I choose as my gift the life of this boy."

The crowd surged to its feet and began to boo and hiss. Walker stared at Draco in horror. There was no way the leader of the Dragons was saving him from death out of the goodness of his heart. He didn't think Lord Draco even had a heart. Lyonel Summerwynd conferred with the man seated next to him. After a few moments, he stood and raised his hand for silence.

"Lord Draco has spoken the truth. It is his right to ask for a gift from me and I cannot refuse, no matter what it is. That is the custom of our land."

The crowd slowly quieted. Walker saw a few heads nod in agreement.

Lyonel Summerwynd turned back to Lord Draco. "The boy is yours," he proclaimed. "To do with what you will . . ."

In the silence that followed, Walker could have sworn he heard the sound of nails being banged into the lid of his coffin one by one.

CHAPTER 16

"Have to rest," Niko said to Topaz as she flew to his shoulder. The cold air made it difficult to breathe.

He had been following his falcon for days, first through the desert, and then through the marshes toward the North. He reached out to stroke her crest feathers, still amazed at their surprising reunion. Together they had traveled day and night, stopping only for an hour's sleep here and there when Niko could no longer put one foot in front of the other. Now, finally, he had come to the Cold Edge. The Dark Peaks rose before him in the distance, and above them towered the Crystal Claw Mountains.

Topaz suddenly turned her head to the right. Niko followed her line of sight. In the moonlight he could see the valley below quite clearly. He could even make out a narrow path, a ribbon of black crossing the silvery landscape, then leading through a dense forest and up the mountain beyond. Topaz cawed once, flew up and landed on Niko's wrist, her talons gripping him, telling him it was time to move on.

Niko pushed himself to a standing position as Topaz flew away again into the dense, dark forest ahead. Niko made his way carefully along the narrow, icy path and stopped just as he reached the towering trees rising up in a thick, dark wall before him. He didn't like forests. Never had. He didn't like being surrounded by trees, unable to see what was ahead or behind. And the noises—the rustling and skittering of animals, or whatever else might lurk in a forest—made him edgy too.

Sighing, he entered the trees. Moonlight cast puddles of silver light, making long wavering shadows through the woods. As the night wind soughed through the leafless branches, Niko felt as if the trees were alive and murmuring all around him. Don't be stupid, he chided himself, but he wished he had a weapon. This forest sat on the far border of civilization, a wild place where wolves roamed and few people could survive. Topaz swooped down, *cak-cak*ing, her yellow eyes urging him onward. Niko gritted his teeth and hurried after her, going deeper into the ancient woods, trying not to think of anything but his quest to find Aurora and the charms.

A sudden howling off in the distance brought him to a stop. Wolves. Out there in the night, hunting for food. With a sharp squawk Topaz plunged toward him.

"What's the matter, girl?" Niko whispered, instantly wary. His bird had alerted him to danger many times in the past.

She flew up, but instead of leading him along the path, she veered into a dense thicket of trees. There was not even a trail that way, and Niko's instinct warned him not to leave the safety of the path, so he took a few more steps along it. But Topaz was insistent, cawing repeatedly. Niko reluctantly left the trail and followed Topaz into the thicket. Little moonlight penetrated the copse, but as Niko's eyes got used to the darkness, he could see a break in the trees up ahead. Cautiously he padded toward it, when he heard the sound of twigs snapping. He stopped and held his breath, listening.

Someone was out there in the forest. Could it be one of the Cold Edge folk who believed in blood sacrifice, or one of the lost tribes of the Skyggni, magic hunters skilled in the ways of black magic, or even a Dragon patrolling the forest?

Minutes passed and nothing moved. It was probably just an animal, Niko reasoned. Slowly he moved forward, but a rustling brought him up short. There *was* someone else in the forest. He ducked down just as a figure, dressed in a bulky hooded cloak and carrying a bundle of sticks, appeared in the clearing ahead. As the figure lit a fire, Niko could see a pinched, pale face and a moon-shaped red scar under the person's right eye. The fire also revealed a shiny object propped against a tree behind the cloaked figure—a sword.

Niko stared at the sword, incredulous, for on its hilt was an engraving he knew well. His heart beat faster in his chest as he gazed at the simple gate symbol. It was his sword, the sword of the valiant warrior Janus, the sword he, Niko, had chosen on a long-ago day at the Castle of the Seven Towers. The sword that was his by right must be his again.

Without pausing, Niko barreled through the trees, his rage against losing Lord Amber, against losing Aurora and then Walker, pumping through his veins. He threw himself on the person who had stolen his sword, pushing him to the snowy forest floor. They rolled over and over, Niko punching the thief in the face and chest as the figure struggled to push Niko off.

Finally, Niko was able to pin the thief to the ground. He pulled back his arm, ready to deliver a harsh blow. "Where did you get that sword?" he demanded.

Before the thief could even answer, someone grabbed Niko around the neck and poked something sharp into his back.

"Let him go or I'll kill you," this new opponent threatened.

Startled, Niko released the cloaked figure, who sprang to his feet and grabbed the sword. Heedless of the knife at his back, Niko shook off his unseen attacker and lunged, managing to wrest the sword from the thief by the sheer force of his rage. As soon as his fingers made contact with the hilt, the air began to hum with energy. A blue white glow lit the dark clearing, revealing the startled faces of Niko, his attacker, and the thief.

"Niko?" blurted out the unseen attacker, just as the thief leaped at the boy.

Niko dodged out of the way, slicing the air with the glowing sword, his eyes transfixed by its shining light.

"Leave him, Serge," the voice said. "It's Niko, the boy I told you about. The Chooser."

Niko turned slowly, unable to believe his ears. "Aurora?" he whispered, staring at the figure behind him. She smiled then and pushed back her hood, her dark curls tumbling around her face.

They ran into each other's arms and embraced, then pulled away to gaze at each other in disbelief.

"What are you doing with this thief?" Niko spit out the words with a sidelong glance at Serge.

"He's not a thief," Aurora said, shaking her head. "He's a friend. He followed me all the way from the City of Sand and Stone. He found the map. It's a long story." And the two companions spent the next hour filling each other in on all that had passed since they separated.

At the end of their stories, Aurora smiled. "I saved one detail for last, Niko. Your master isn't dead. The Dragons captured Lord Amber and took him to Nine Shadows Henge. He's fine—except that they burned out one of his eyes. But really, he's okay, and he said the most important thing was for me to find you, and I did."

Niko didn't say anything for a long moment. "My master is alive!" he exclaimed finally. "Lord Amber is alive! We have to go to Nine Shadows Henge and rescue him."

"But first we have to get more rope and some better grappling hooks," Serge said, speaking for the first time. "The only way into that place without being seen is to climb the outer tower walls, and the only way to do that is with hooks and a lot of rope."

Niko nodded at the wisdom of Serge's suggestion. "I'm sorry about attacking you," he apologized with a shrug.

"It's okay," Serge said.

"Where are we going to get supplies?" Niko asked.

"There's an outpost—the last one before the mountains," Serge replied. "We better get there now and get what we need." With that, he stamped out their fire and headed out of the clearing.

"Right. Then we have to free Lord Amber," Niko said, almost more to himself than the others, gritting his teeth in determination as they followed Serge through the forest.

"No," Aurora countered, "Lord Amber told me that we have to stop the black dragon from rising." She looked into Niko's eyes. "He was very clear about that."

"Without the charms, this black dragon can't rise, right?" Serge asked. "And then that evil sorcerer won't be released from that cage the Lords of Time trapped him in. What was his name?"

"Malachite," Aurora replied. The three lapsed into silence, the only sound the crunching of snow beneath their feet. Finally they came to the simple wooden structure of the outpost. From inside came the sound of laughter, the clanking of tankards, and the smell of smoke.

Niko stopped and turned to Aurora, his gray eyes dark. "You're sure Lord Amber said that we should get the charms first?"

"Yes," Aurora replied without hesitation.

Niko knew that Aurora was telling the truth. The more he thought about it, the more the command sounded like Lord Amber—the charms first, even before his own life.

"Listen," Serge whispered, "we have to be careful in there and keep our eyes out for those magic hunters and for Dragons." His fingers strayed unconsciously to the three purple dots on his cheek. Niko looked away, remembering what Aurora had told him about Lavandula, and shuddered.

Serge pushed open the weather-beaten door. Heat and smoke enveloped them like a cloud as they stepped inside. The place was crowded with people sitting at tables or clustered around a long wooden bar at the far end.

"Now what?" Niko whispered, glancing around nervously.

"Climbing supplies are behind the bar," Serge said. "We'll just slip over there real quietly, buy them from the matron, and leave."

Niko's eyes widened as a terrible thought struck him. "But how are we going to pay for them? We don't have any money."

"I do," Serge said, pulling a gold juno out of his pocket. "Now let's get this over with before anyone notices us. Between the Dragons and Lavandula, I have a feeling we're a little too welcome for our own good."

Quickly the three pushed through the crowd toward the bar. Elbowing his way between two of the fur-clad patrons, Niko heard Serge ask for the supplies. He and Aurora stood behind, trying not to meet anyone's eyes. As the wrinkled old woman behind the bar was about to hand Serge the rope, she spotted Niko, or rather she noticed his sword. Her brown eyes grew hard as she stared at his fine weapon. She pointed to it, gesturing with her gnarled fingers for the men at the bar to look at it too.

"Where did you get that, boy?" The old crone's voice was shrill and sharp, cutting through the noise of the bar like a knife.

All eyes turned to Niko.

"Wh-what?" he stammered.

"That sword," the woman said, pointing with a crooked forefinger. "I've seen that sword before—a long time ago—but I've never seen you."

Niko felt Aurora's sympathetic presence beside him, but there was nothing she could do. "Um . . . it was given to me by . . ." Niko's voice trailed off as he tried to think of a good lie this woman would believe, but as he was a truthful boy, lying did not come at all easily to him. ". . . by my uncle."

The crowd murmured, then the crone spoke again in her shrill, piercing voice. "I don't believe you, boy. That is too fine a sword for the likes of you."

Niko bit his lip as Aurora nudged Serge. "Let's go," she whispered. "Forget the rope. You can come back for it later."

"Where'd you get it, boy?" one of the men shouted, banging his tankard against the bar and glaring at Niko.

"It's his sword, honest," Serge cut in before Niko could speak. "He comes from a noble family in the City of Sand and Stone. He's just been on a journey, a quest, and I came along to guide him, you know."

More murmuring rippled through the crowd as they digested this information.

"Let's go," Aurora urged Niko, just as one of the fur-clad men at the bar leaped for the sword, his yellow teeth bared in a nasty grin.

"Gimme it," he demanded, grabbing for the sword.

Without thinking, Niko yanked the sword out of the man's grasp with the same blind rage that had surged through his veins with Serge. Once again it began to glow and hum, filling the tense smoky silence of the bar.

"The prophecy . . . ," someone whispered.

"Strange things have been happening," the old woman remarked in a shocked voice. "The blue wolf has been spotted in the mountains, and now the Chooser has come bearing the silver sword."

Quickly Serge shoved his golden juno at the old crone and took the rope and the hooks. The crowd parted in continued silence as Niko led the way out, bearing the brilliant sword.

CHAPTER 17

"So this is the Bearer of the Light," remarked a rasping and oddly inhuman voice.

"Yes, Malachite," Lord Draco answered, moving closer to the black iron cage that held the source of the voice.

"You have done well, Lord Draco," praised the ancient voice, freezing Walker's insides. "And soon you shall ascend your throne and assume your birthright as the last of the great black dragon kings. And I, the Sorcerer of the Dark, shall be released from the bonds that have kept me trapped in this cage after all these centuries. The light stands no chance against us. Finally, our time has come."

Lord Draco bowed respectfully and moved to stand by the door.

"Step closer, Bearer of the Light," the eerie voice said. "Step closer so that I can see your face. And so you can see mine."

Walker stood frozen, his entire body rebelling against the idea of moving even an inch nearer the voice in that cage.

"Do not be afraid—I will not hurt you. You are much too important to the proceedings to be done away with—yet. You are the first one chosen, and were it not for you, the time of the prophecy would not be at hand. Now come."

Walker forced himself forward, seeing no other alternative.

"Look into my eyes, Bearer of the Light," the evil voice commanded.

Walker felt his head rise against his will, unable to resist. What he saw was so unexpected, he blinked to clear his vision. Sitting in the cage was a little boy with blond curly hair and dimples in his cheeks. But clearly this was no ordinary child—no boy could have glowing yellow eyes like that. Walker shuddered, but those horrible eyes held him fast, and suddenly he felt himself being lifted off the ground, propelled upward by an invisible force. He tried to push himself back down, but he was powerless to stop the force just as he was powerless to look away from those horrible yellow eyes. With a sudden whoosh, his head hit the ceiling, and a cold, dark feeling gripped him. He felt as if all hope and all happiness were being drained out of him, and somewhere he thought he could hear the sound of his mother crying, and he thought he could see the body of his dog, Blue, dead and broken, eyes vacant and staring at nothing. "No!" gasped Walter as with another whoosh he was hurled across the room and fell to the floor. He shook his head to clear it, his heart pounding as he staggered to his feet.

"Now you have had a taste of the power of the dark. Do not even try to avoid doing what you must, for there are worse things than death, Bearer of the Light, and they will be yours if you defy the prophecy."

"Where is the Bearer of the Dark?" the ancient voice of Malachite echoed in the silent room as the boy turned his gaze from Walker to Draco.

Lord Draco motioned to the Dragon nearest him, and the door of the room opened, letting in two girls.

"Elyana!" Walker cried. "What are you doing here?"

Elyana turned at the sound of her name, but her blank eyes looked at him and then away, showing no sign of recognition. She wore the same vacant expression she'd had at the trial.

"Not that there is any need for you to know, but I will tell you this much," Lord Draco said, training his dark eyes on Walker. "She is here at my request. After all, she is my fiancée, and her father felt it quite appropriate that she come to see her new homeland." Lord Draco smiled coldly at his own words.

Walker glared at Zoe, anger burning through his veins. "What have you done to her, you double-crossing, lying little—"

"Come to me, Bearer of the Dark, bearer of the charm of air and ice," Malachite intoned, as if Walker had not spoken. His yellow eyes were fastened on Zoe. "The blue charm. The coldest of colors. The light of day that becomes the light of night."

Lord Draco bowed and nodded for Zoe to step forward.

Zoe walked over to Malachite with a toss of her shiny, dark hair. On the way she managed to shoot Walker a look of disdain, as if he were something slimy she'd found on the bottom of her shoe.

"You have done well, Bearer of the Dark," purred Malachite. "You have delivered both the charm of fire and blood and the last of the line of the white dragon."

"So can I go back to my world now?" Zoe asked.

"You have one more task," Malachite said. "One more step to take in order for the dark to gain ascendancy over the light. You, the Bearer of the Dark, must place the nine charms in the pattern of the dragon. Only then will the black dragon be released."

"But I don't know anything about a pattern," Zoe said slowly.

"It will be revealed at its proper time. Then, if you choose to return to your world, you may. But you will have to wait and see what your heart truly desires at that time."

Walker barely noticed Zoe bow and return to her position next to Elyana. He thought about the mosaic back in the tower of the white dragon and of the symbols he'd scratched on the piece of leather hidden under his belt. And he remembered that other pattern, the one he'd seen illuminated by the light, the hidden pattern. He visualized the sequence of simple symbols in the plume of fire and suddenly thought of something. The beginnings of a plan stirred in his mind.

"Soon I will be released," Malachite continued in his eerie voice, his yellow eyes trained on Lord Draco, "freed from this cage in which the Lords of Time trapped me so many centuries ago, as well as from the prison of this child's body. With the first screams of the black dragon I shall assume my true and powerful form. After that, I will unite the black dragon king and his bride-to-be, the last of the white dragon lineage."

Malachite's eyes sought Elyana, whose gaze remained riveted on the floor.

"Then shall your child, the heir of the blood of the black and the white dragon thrones, rule both the light and the dark."

"What!" Walker shouted, forgetting in the heat of the moment his status as a prisoner. "You can't do that. She's just a girl. She doesn't want to marry an old man like Lord Draco. Anyway, she's drugged or something so she doesn't even know what's going on."

Malachite turned his burning yellow gaze on Walker but said nothing. Then he swung his blond curly head back toward Lord Draco and smiled, showing the dimples in his round, baby cheeks. "Soon it will be time. . . ."

"There they are," Aurora murmured with awe as she pointed at the purple velvet pouch, which had been placed on a massive gray stone slab. It was circled by nine huge standing stones, each one linked to the other by crosspieces of stone placed on top.

"What is this place?" Niko asked.

"It's where the charms used to be kept when the Lords of Time still lived," Aurora said.

"I feel as if I know this place," Niko said in a far-away voice, "as if I've been here before. Or maybe someone I know has been here and told me about it."

"I don't like it," Serge whispered. "Leaving the charms unguarded like that doesn't make sense."

Aurora nodded, wondering if Serge was right. She was tired and couldn't really think straight. The climb up had been hard. At least she had remembered the way into this dim, cavernous room beneath the tower, where the charms had been the last time. And at least they were here, as she had hoped. Now all they had to do was take the pouch and then go to the tower and rescue Lord Amber.

"It's almost as if they want us to take the charms," Serge continued.

"You might be right," Aurora agreed. "Last time it was a trap." She and Serge both stared at the purple velvet pouch, glowing in the light of the torches placed around the stone on which they sat.

"But I think the reason they put the charms here has something to do with the old magic of this place. Maybe their powers get stronger from being around these old stones. I don't know."

Niko stood up suddenly, his eyes on the pouch.

"Niko," Aurora whispered, "what are you doing?"

"These stones . . . this place . . . ," Niko said dreamily as he moved out of the shadows into the light. "I know I've been here. . . ." With one hand he stroked the surface of the rough gray stone. "It was many, many years ago."

"Niko, get out of the light!" Aurora shouted as she ran toward him, closely followed by Serge.

Before any of them could say another word, ropes fell from the shadowy recesses of the high vaulted ceiling. Within an instant, Dragons dressed in the bloodred of the House of the Black Rock surrounded them.

"Sister, I see that you've returned," Jah said with a cold smile. "And once again you have helped the black dragon and the Sorcerer of the Dark." He turned quickly to one of the Dragons behind him. "Tell Lord Draco that our guests have arrived."

"She has done nothing for the dark or for the black dragon," Niko cut in, his gray eyes flashing. "You are mistaken, Dragon."

"So you think, Chooser. But then again, you know nothing, just like your master, that ignorant, senile old fool who fancies himself a sorcerer." Jah walked toward the offering stone and picked up the purple velvet pouch. "She has indeed done much for the dark. Without her we would not be here, would we?"

Aurora stared at Jah, filled with anger and something worse, between fear and horror. She began to breathe slowly, air in one nostril and out the other. Jah turned toward her, and she saw that he, too, was breathing the breath of the Old Ones, the breath of power.

"I am also trained in the arts of mind control, sister," he said.

She felt him enter her mind with a slamming rush, searching for the source of her will. And no matter how she tried to resist him, she could not overpower the wave of his mind as he probed deeper and deeper. Within a moment blackness descended on her. Aurora's mouth opened and closed but no words came out.

"The power of the light can always be vanquished by that of the dark, did you not know that, sister?" Jah intoned in his calm, flat voice. "It is as inevitable as the night, so do not fight it, for you will surely lose."

CHAPTER 18

Dreadful anticipation filled Walker as he followed Lord Draco, Elyana and Zoe, and four Dragons carrying Malachite's cage down a long, dark set of stairs, stopping finally in front of the tallest double doors he had ever seen. The Dragon's Eye was emblazoned in the center of the wooden doors.

Walker blinked when he entered the lofty chamber. As his eyes grew accustomed to the glare of the torchlight, he started in surprise.

"Niko!" he shouted, raising a hand toward his friend who was flanked by Dragon guards. Next to him stood a girl with long dark hair and a boy with a moon-shaped scar under his eye. Clearly all three were captives of the Dragons.

"And so we are gathered at last," Lord Draco intoned as he led Walker, Elyana, and Zoe toward the massive stone slab inside the circle of tall stones. "The Protector . . ." Lord Draco sought out the girl with the dark hair. "The Chooser . . ." He turned then to Niko. "The Bearer of the Light . . ." Walker blanched under the cold, black gaze as those fanatical eyes turned to him. "The Bearer of the Dark . . ." Zoe smiled. "And dearest of all to my heart, the white dragon queen." His glance lingered on Elyana, her green eyes vague and unfocused. Walker clenched his hand into a fist.

At a nod from Lord Draco, the four Dragons bearing Malachite's cage stepped forward and placed it on the other side of the central stone. There was silence as Malachite trained his yellow eyes on Zoe. "The time has finally come to release the black dragon," he began in his ancient voice. "As the prophecy says,

> *But if a second Bearer*
> *by the dark is then called forth,*
> *the black dragon shall be freed*
> *from its prison in the North."*

Malachite stared at Walker as he spoke the rest.

> *"And the Bearer of the Dark*
> *shall face the Bearer of the Light.*

The white dragon must be risen
or all shall be endless night.

"And so the time has come, as it was long ago fore-told, for the black dragon to rise. Because the charms are in the possession of the dark, there is no hope for you to release the white dragon, especially once I have been freed from the bonds of the light. Now let the ceremony begin."

How were he and Zoe supposed to face off? Walker wondered as he watched Lord Draco move closer to the central stone and pick up the velvet pouch. Carefully he poured the contents onto the stone surface. The gemstones gleamed all the colors of the rainbow, casting a brighter light than the blazing torches around them.

"Bring forth the Bearer of the Light," Lord Draco commanded. A Dragon grabbed Walker, leading him to the center.

"Bearer of the Light," Lord Draco thundered, "from you shall come the pattern that will release the dragon."

Walker thought of the two patterns he'd noticed in the white dragon mosaic. One of them, he figured, must be the pattern that would release the black dragon—the question was, which one?

"The prophecy is clear. If the Bearer of the Light places the charms in the correct pattern, then the white dragon will be released. But if the Bearer of the Dark places the charms, then the black dragon will be freed."

So it hadn't been an accident that Walker had seen the pattern in the white dragon mosaic. According to the prophecy he was supposed to do that. The more he considered what he knew, he felt that his plan was worth a try. He thought of the leather with the pattern he'd carved, and then he thought of the secret pattern, running over the symbols in his mind—cross, triangle, asterisk, square, on to the final one of the half circle. All he had to do was fake them out by pretending the pattern on the leather was the pattern of the dragon, and not the other one, the hidden one, that he was pretty sure was the true one. He crossed his fingers, hoping against hope that he was right and that his plan might work. It might not stop Lord Draco and the Sorcerer of the Dark entirely, but it might at least buy some time.

"And now, Bearer of the Light, reveal to us the pattern of the dragon," Lord Draco commanded, his black eyes on Walker. "Then the Bearer of the Dark will place the charms and the black dragon will rise."

Walker took a deep breath, thinking of what he knew, as he forced himself to return Lord Draco's triumphant stare.

"The pattern, Bearer of the Light," prodded the commanding voice.

Walker took a deep breath. "I don't know what you

mean," he said, fixing Lord Draco with his most innocent stare and shrugging as if he were confused.

"Don't play games with me."

"I'm not," Walker said, opening his eyes wide as if
he didn't have a clue. Then, knowing that the Dragon
named Jah had been watching his every move, he
glanced quickly down at his belt, where the piece of
leather was hidden. As Jah's green-and-yellow-flecked
cat eyes met his, Walker looked away guiltily, as if he
had been caught doing something he didn't want anybody to know. In one swift movement Jah grabbed
Walker's belt, and the piece of leather fell to the
ground. Jah smiled as he picked it up.

"Here is the pattern of the dragon, Lord Draco,"
Jah said.

Walker watched in tense silence as Jah offered the
piece of leather to Lord Draco. But before Lord Draco
had even touched it, Malachite spoke.

"Very clever, Bearer, but we want the true pattern."

The girl with the dark hair began to wave her arms
wildly in Walker's direction. "Close your mind!" she
shouted. "Don't let him in! No matter what you do,
don't think about what you know!"

Malachite's yellow eyes gleamed as he turned to the
girl, the hint of a smile on his baby face. "It doesn't
matter, Protector, for I already know the pattern, just as
I know the secrets lurking in *your* mind—such as your

promise to rescue my old rival, Lord Amber, the Sorcerer of the Light."

The girl stared at Malachite, unable to hide the surprise on her face.

"Ah, you were not aware of the subtlety of my probing. Now you know. The secrets of the light are not safe from me—or from the dark."

Malachite then trained his terrible eyes on Walker. "Thank you, Bearer of the Light. You have done exactly as predicted, finding those hidden symbols in the mosaic of the white dragon. I applaud you."

Lord Draco inclined his dark head in Zoe's direction. "Bearer of the Dark, step forward."

Walker watched as Zoe walked calmly toward the center stone, her head high, as if she were the head Laker girl at the final play-off game, leading the other cheerleaders.

"The black dragon shall now be risen," Malachite proclaimed from his cage, his eyes burning an even brighter yellow.

Lord Draco proceeded to pick up the red charm. Then Malachite pointed to one of the standing stones.

"Bearer of the Dark," Lord Draco intoned, giving the charm to Zoe. "Place this where the Dark Sorcerer wishes."

Walker peered at the stone, struggling to see how Malachite knew it was the right one. And there it was—

the first symbol hidden in the dragon fire of the mosaic—the square. It was cut into the stone, just above eye level, deep enough to hold the charm. Zoe moved toward the tall stone, bearing the red charm faceup on her palm, with a smug, self-satisfied look on her face, clearly enjoying all the attention.

Zoe reached up and gently placed the charm in the square-shaped recess. As soon as she stepped away, there was a rumbling jolt and the ground shook. Walker shifted uneasily, trying to catch Niko's eye, but he was blocked by one of the stones. If only he could think of something, anything, to stop the horrible proceedings. Walker watched helplessly as Lord Draco next handed Zoe her own charm, the icy blue one. Again Malachite pointed to the standing stone where he wanted it placed. This stone had a triangle engraved into it, the shape Walker remembered as second in the column of symbols.

Zoe carefully slid the blue charm into its niche, and the earth rumbled once more. Walker's heart began to beat faster. Was the whole place going to come down around their ears because of this ceremony? Even the Dragons shifted uneasily. But Lord Draco and Malachite didn't seem at all disturbed. And Zoe maintained the imperious poise of an actress performing a part for an audience who loved her. She went on to place the third charm at Malachite's direction, its yellow gem winking in the torchlight. And then the fourth. The earth continued to rumble, and in the distance somewhere far below it sounded as if the very stones of the mountain were being prized loose. Zoe placed the purple charm without missing a step, although Walker noticed a flicker of apprehension cross her face at a particularly loud rumble.

Nevertheless, she placed the coral charm and then the gleaming black onyx. After that, Lord Draco handed her the eighth charm, which was pearly white, and she placed it in the niche Malachite indicated. Suddenly rocks began to fall from the ceiling. Only one charm remained. This one had a dark blue stone in its center, so dark it looked almost black. Midnight blue. Walker watched in horror as Zoe bore the ninth and final charm to the last of the standing stones.

At the same time, a sudden movement caught Aurora's eye. At first she thought it was just a shadow, but as she squinted in the dim light, she saw that someone on all fours was crawling toward one of the standing stones. She stared, wondering, as the person slowly got up. She could just make out a glint of fair hair—it was Serge. He had slipped away from her and Niko without either of them noticing. She watched out of the corner of her eye so as not to draw attention to him. He was reaching up toward the niche in which the yellow charm had been placed. Just as he went for it, a flash of blue white light shot out at him and he fell backward. No one else saw what had happened, because at the same moment the bars of Malachite's cage burst open. Aurora's mouth opened in a wide *O* of horror. Where the small blond boy had been now stood a tall, hunchbacked old man, his lined face creased into a terrible grimace, his fingers crooked like claws. But worst of all were his eyes—they now burned with a reddish glow.

In the distance a horrible screeching echoed through Nine Shadows Henge, a sound that sent shivers up and down Aurora's spine. Accompanying the freeing of the Dark Sorcerer and the bellowing of the black dragon was a massive rumbling, and the floor began to break apart. Huge cracks opened up in the stone surface, and rocks cascaded down the crumbling walls. Panic filled the room, and everyone began running at once, trying to escape without being crushed to death by the falling stones. Aurora caught a glimpse of Lord Draco herding Elyana and Zoe out of the room. Dragon guards rushed back and forth, their red robes blurring in the gloom.

Just then she felt someone grab her by the arm. "Let's go!" Niko shouted as Walker came running toward them.

"What about Elyana?" Walker yelled over the din.

"Draco took her and the Bearer of the Dark some-where," Aurora shouted back.

"We can't do anything for her now," Niko yelled. "We'd better get out of here."

"Where's Serge?" Aurora asked, staring around frantically, wondering what had happened to him.

"There he is!" Niko called, pointing toward the center stone.

Serge was backing away from the Dark Sorcerer, whose evil eyes were riveted angrily on the boy.

"This way, Serge!" Aurora shouted as Jah and two of the Dragon guards rushed toward him.

"Get that boy!" Malachite bellowed, his eyes burning yellow red in the darkness.

But Serge was too fast for them. He jumped across a widening crack in the floor, barreling toward the wide entranceway where the double doors, now shattered, had hung. Niko, Walker, and Aurora took off after him, through the doors and up the circular stairs. At the top Aurora glanced back and saw a flash of red.

"Faster!" she urged the others.

Panting for breath, the four of them hurtled along one dark hallway after another, lost in the maze of passages of Nine Shadows Henge. But no matter how fast they ran, Jah and the Dragons were there, just behind them.

Suddenly Serge dodged to the right, through a broken door into a storage room filled with jars and boxes, and the others followed. They all hunkered down behind some crates, trying to catch their breath as quietly as possible. A minute passed. The silence rang in Aurora's ears, and she realized that the horrible shrieking of the dragon had stopped. Before she could think of what that might mean, she heard voices shouting and footsteps coming toward them.

Aurora hoped the Dragons would keep going. She kept her mind as blank as possible so that Jah could not sense her presence. Nothing happened for a moment, then they heard someone enter the room. The four of them froze, holding their breath. Whoever it was must not have noticed anything, for after a few seconds the person left. As soon as the sound of footsteps faded away, Serge nodded, and the four of them made their way back out into the hall. No one was in sight. But then, just like in a nightmare, Jah and the Dragons burst out from around the opposite corner.

"Run!" Walker cried.

The four of them took off toward a door at the other end of the hall. Niko and Walker reached it at the same time, but it wouldn't open. Niko ran back and jumped, kicking at the door with his foot. It burst open. Aurora and Serge put on a final burst of speed and followed Niko and Walker into the freezing night. Somehow they had emerged where the rock foundation of Nine Shadows Henge met the edge of a dark forest.

"We can lose them in the forest!" Niko shouted, leading the way toward the trees.

But the trees were so densely grown together they'd have to be hacked away with a sword. The companions would never make it through. Aurora turned back, her stomach lurching. Jah and the Dragons were less than two strides away.

"This time I will not let you go, sister," Jah declared.

His green eyes moved from her to Serge, and he glared at the boy. Aurora frowned, wondering why Serge angered him so much. She felt a strange connection with Jah just then, felt his rage at something Serge had done. But what? Malachite seemed to want Serge more than the rest of them, but why? In the split second she was inside Jah's mind, he brushed past her toward Serge.

"Run, Serge! Run!" Aurora screamed.

Jah grabbed for Serge, with the other two Dragons just behind him. But as his fingers closed on the gray wool of Serge's cloak, something lunged out of the forest. A wolf! As Aurora watched in horror, the beast opened its great mouth, revealing rows of sharp white teeth, and began to howl.

"The blue wolf!" shouted a Dragon, his voice cracking in fear.

The Dragons turned and ran. The blue wolf stared first at Niko and Walker, then at Serge, and finally at Aurora. They all stared back, frozen in place as if held by invisible threads.

"Run!" Walker croaked.

But Aurora knew it wouldn't matter. They stood no real chance against the muscular beast before them. As they took off she braced herself for the crush of the wolf on top of her, for the pain of his jaws severing the tendons of her neck.

The attack never came. Instead, the wolf leaped over them with one magnificent jump and pursued the Dragons. Aurora watched in shock as the wolf leaped first on one Dragon and then another, forcing them to the ground. Jah was nowhere in sight.

And then the beast came trotting back toward the four of them, his great jowls dripping blood. Aurora steeled herself. Now it was their turn. But instead of attacking, the blue wolf lay down at their feet.

The four companions stared at each other, their eyes wide in shock, before looking down at the massive, shaggy blue animal. Serge glanced at each of them in turn as a slow grin spread across his face.

"What are you smiling at?" Walker asked.

"Look what I got," Serge said. He opened his hand. In his palm lay something gleaming with a not-quite-silver, not-quite-gold sheen—the yellow charm.

The three of them stared in surprise.

"So that's why they were after you," Walker said. "How'd you manage that?"

Serge shrugged but didn't answer. Aurora stole a glance at him out of the corner of her eye and smiled.

"You did it because you're the Thief," she said.

"What?" Serge replied, a look of mock hurt in his eyes. "Me? A thief?"

"That's what Lord Amber told me. He said that someone known as 'the Thief' would steal the one thing that we needed more than any other."

Aurora looked at Niko just as his gray eyes met hers. The Chooser and the Protector knew then just what they must do. And at that moment, as if she did too, Topaz swooped down from the cold night sky and landed on Niko's shoulder, her eyes on the yellow charm that gleamed in the darkness like a beacon, leading them on to their next adventure.

ABOUT THE AUTHORS

ERICA FARBER is a children's book editor turned writer who has always believed in the possibility of other worlds. She has kept journals since she was eleven, trying to remember all the important things that kids know but grown-ups forget.

J. R. SANSEVERE is a twenty-year veteran of the children's entertainment industry, involved in everything from books to videos to CD-ROMs. He has collaborated on many projects with author and illustrator Mercer Mayer, including award-winning computer programming for kids.

THE TALES OF THE NINE CHARMS trilogy was inspired by Eastern philosophy and quantum physics, both of which suggest that the cosmic dance of energy, or the ebb and flow of particles, leaves open the possibility that other worlds exist. Here is the authors' vision of one possible world.